Muriel Spark was born and educated in Edinburgh, and spent some years in Central Africa. She returned to Britain during the war and worked in the Political Intelligence Department of the Foreign Office. She subsequently edited two poetry magazines, and her published works include critical biographies of nineteenth-century figures and editions of nineteenth-century letters. Her *Collected Poems I* and *Collected Stories I* were published in 1967. Since she won an *Observer* short-story competition in 1951 her creative writings have achieved international recognition (they are published in twenty different languages). Among many other awards she has received the Italia Prize and the James Tait Black Memorial Prize. She was awarded the O.B.E. in 1967 and she became an Honorary Member of the American Academy of Arts and Letters in 1978.

Mrs Spark became a Roman Catholic in 1954. She has one son.

Her first novel, *The Comforters*, was published in 1957 and this was followed by *Robinson* (1958), *The Go-Away Bird and Other Stories* (1958), *Memento Mori* (1959), *The Ballad of Peckham Rye* (1960), *The Bachelors* (1960), *Voices at Play* (1961), *The Prime of Miss Jean Brodie* (1961), adaptations of which have enjoyed long and successful runs on the West End stage and the screen, *The Girls of Slender Means* (1963), *The Mandelbaum Gate* (1965), *The Public Image* (1968), *The Driver's Seat* (1970), *Not to Disturb* (1971), *The Hothouse by the East River* (1973), *The Abbess of Crewe* (1974), *The Takeover* (1976), *Territorial Rights* (1979), *Loitering with Intent* (1981), *Bang-Bang You're Dead and Other Stories* (1982), a volume of poems, *Going Up to Sotheby's* (1982), and *The Only Problem* (1984).

Her play, *Doctors of Philosophy*, was first produced in London in 1962 and published in 1963.

MURIEL SPARK

ROBINSON

PENGUIN BOOKS

Penguin Books Ltd, Harmondsworth, Middlesex, England
Viking Penguin Inc., 40 West 23rd Street, New York, New York 10010, U.S.A.
Penguin Books Australia Ltd, Ringwood, Victoria, Australia
Penguin Books Canada Limited, 2801 John Street, Markham, Ontario, Canada L3R 1B4
Penguin Books (N.Z.) Ltd, 182–190 Wairau Road, Auckland 10, New Zealand

—

First published by Macmillan 1958
Published in Penguin Books 1964
Reprinted 1978, 1982, 1987

—

—

Printed and bound in Great Britain by
Cox & Wyman Ltd, Reading
Set in Monotype Baskerville

For My Mother and Father
With Love

ROBINSON

84 SQ MILES

THE NORTH LEG

THE NORTH KNEE

THE NORTH ARM

Vasco da Gama's Bay

Shark Bay

THE WEST LEG

The Mountain

THE HEADLANDS

The Pomegranate Bay

South Arm Bay

THE SOUTH ARM

1 Wrecked Plane
2 Robinson's House
3 Blue & Green Lake
4 Mustard Field
5&6 Paths to Snow-White Beach
7 Snow-White Beach
8 13&18 Secret Tunnels
9 Derelict Croft & Mill
10 Burial Ground
11 The Market
12 Sheer Cliffs
14 The Furnace
15 Pomegranate Plantations
16,17 Lava Boulders
19 Pasture Land

Chapter 1

IF you ask me how I remember the island, what it was like to be stranded there by misadventure for nearly three months, I would answer that it was a time and landscape of the mind if I did not have the visible signs to summon its materiality: my journal, the cat, the newspaper cuttings, the curiosity of my friends; and my sisters — how they always look at me, I think, as one returned from the dead.

You have read about the incident in the papers, and there were some aerial pictures of the island which, when I saw them later, were difficult to recognize as the scene of all I am going to tell you. Most of all, it is the journal that gives me my bearings. It fetches before me the play of thought and action hidden amongst the recorded facts. Through my journal I nearly came by my death.

Three of us were projected from the blazing plane when it crashed on Robinson's island. We were the only survivors of twenty-nine souls including the crew, and, as you know, we were presumed lost until we were found two months and twenty-nine days later. I had concussion and a dislocated left shoulder. Jimmie Waterford got off with a few cuts and bruises. Tom Wells had fractured ribs. I made a quick recovery, and had not been ten days on the island when I started my journal in a damp paper exercise-book which Robinson gave me for the purpose. I see that I began by writing my name, the place, and the date, as follows:

January Marlow,
Robinson
May 20, 1954

My name is January, because I was born in January. I

7

would like to state that I am never called Jan although some of the Sunday papers used that name on their headlines when the news came out that we had been picked up.

Robinson thought at the time that keeping a journal would be an occupation for my mind, and I fancied that I might later dress it up for a novel. That was most peculiar, as things transpired, for I did not then anticipate how the journal would turn upon me, so that, having survived the plane disaster, I should nearly meet my death through it.

Sometimes I am a little vague about the details of the day before yesterday until some word or thing, almost a sacramental, touches my memory, and then the past comes walking over me as we say an angel is walking over our grave, and I stand in the past as in the beam of a searchlight.

When I looked through my island journal again, quite recently, I came across the words, 'Robinson played Rossini to us on his gramophone.' I remembered then, not only Robinson's addiction to Rossini, but all that was in my mind on that evening. That was the twenty-fifth of June, not long before Robinson disappeared. I recall that night – it was my seventh week on the island – I left Robinson's house and climbed down the mountain track among the blue gum trees to the coast. It was a warm night, free from mist, full of moon. I had a desire to throw wide my arms and worship the moon. 'But,' I thought to myself, 'I am a Christian.' Still I had this sweet and dreadful urge towards the moon, and I went back indoors slightly disturbed.

Lying awake that night on my mattress I remembered that my grandmother from Hertfordshire used to recite a little rhyme to the new moon, no matter where, or in what busy street she might be. I saw her in my mind's eye, as I see her now, setting herself apart on the road, intent on the pale crescent against the deepening northern sky:

> New Moon, New Moon, be good to me,
> And bring me presents, one, two, three.

8

Then she would bow three times. 'One,' she repeated. 'Two. Three.' As a child it embarrassed me if I chanced to be out with her at new moon. I dreaded every moment that one of my school chums might come along and find me associated with this eccentric behaviour. I ramble on, for I am still a little intoxicated with the memory of my sudden wanting to worship the moon among the tall blue gums and sleeping bougainvillaea, with the sea at my ears. I was the only woman on the island, and it is said the pagan mind runs strong in women at any time, let alone on an island, and such an island. It is not only the moon, the incident, that I am thinking of. I consider now how my perceptions during that whole period were touched with a pre-ancestral quality, how there was an enchantment, a primitive blood-force which probably moved us all.

Sometimes people say to me, 'If only you hadn't undertaken that journey . . .' 'What a pity you didn't catch an earlier plane . . .' or 'To think that you nearly went by sea!'

I am inclined to reject the idea behind these remarks in the same way as I reject the idea that it is best to have never been born.

The plane crashed on the tenth of May, 1954. It had been bound for the Azores but missed the airport of Santa Maria in the fog. I woke by the side of a green and blue mountain lake, and immediately thought, 'The banana boat must have been wrecked.' I then went back into my coma.

It is true I had nearly taken a banana boat bound for the West Indies which called in at the Azores, but had been gradually dissuaded by my friends, after we had taken several looks at the Lascars, Danes, and Irish lolling round the East India Docks. And so, although I had finally taken the expensive Lisbon route by plane, still in my dreams it was the banana boat.

When I came round the second time it was in Robinson's

9

house. I was lying on a mattress on the floor, and as I moved I felt my shoulder hurting very painfully. I could see, facing me through the misty sunlight of a partly open door, a corner of the blue and green lake. We seemed to be quite high on the side of a mountain.

I could hear someone moving in an inner room to my left. In a few moments I heard the voices of two men.

'I say!' I called out. The voices stopped. Then one murmured something.

Presently a door opened at my left. I tried to twist round, but this was painful, and I waited while a man entered the room and came to face me.

'Where am I?'

'Robinson,' he said.

'*Where?*'

'Robinson.'

He was short and square, with a brown face and greyish curly hair.

'Robinson,' he repeated. 'In the North Atlantic Ocean. How do you feel?'

'Who are you?'

'Robinson,' he said. 'How do you feel?'

'*Who?*'

'Robinson.'

'I think I must be suffering from concussion,' I said.

He said, 'I'm glad you think so, because it is true. To know you have concussion, when you have it, is one-third of the cure. I see you are intelligent.'

On hearing this I decided that I liked Robinson, and settled down to sleep. He shook me awake and placed at my lips a mug of warm tangy milk. While I gulped it, he said,

'Sleep is another third of the cure, and nourishment is the remaining third.'

'My shoulder hurts,' I said.

'Which shoulder?'

I touched my left shoulder. I found it stiff with bandages.

'Which shoulder?' he said.

'This one,' I said, 'it is bound up.'

'*Which* shoulder? Don't point. Think. Describe.'

I paused for light. Presently I said, 'My left shoulder.'

'That's true. You will soon recover.'

A little fluffy blue-grey cat came and sat in the open doorway, squinting at me as I fell asleep.

This was twenty hours after the crash. When I woke again it was dark and I was frightened.

'I say!' I called out.

No reply, and so, after a few minutes, I called out again, 'I say, Robinson!'

A soft living thing jumped on my chest. I screamed, I sat up despite the pain which the movement caused my shoulder. My hand touched soft fur as the cat sprang off the mattress.

Robinson came in with an oil lamp and peered down at me under its beam.

'I thought it was a rat,' I said, 'but it was the cat.'

He placed the lamp on a shiny table. 'Did you feel afraid?' he said.

'Oh, I'm quite tough. But first there was the darkness and then the cat. I thought it was a rat.'

He bent and stroked the cat which was arching around his legs. 'Her name's Bluebell,' he said and went out.

I heard him moving about, and presently he was back with some hot spicy soup. He looked tired, and sighed a little as he gave it to me.

'What is your name?' he said.

'January Marlow.'

'Think,' he said. 'Try to think.'

'Think of what?'

'Your name.'

'January Marlow,' I said, and placed the mug of soup on the floor beside me.

He lifted the mug and replaced it in my right hand.

'Sip it, and meanwhile think. You have told me the month and place of your birth. What is your name?'

I was rather pleased about his mistake, it gave me confidence.

'I am called by the unusual name of January because I was born in –'

Immediately he understood. 'Oh yes, I see.'

'You thought it was my concussion,' I said.

He smiled feebly.

Suddenly I said, 'There must have been an accident. I was on the Lisbon plane.'

I sipped the broth while I tried to elucidate what my statement had implied.

'Don't think too hard,' Robinson said, 'all at one time.'

'I remember the Lisbon plane,' I said.

'Were you with friends or relations?'

I knew the answer to that. 'No,' I said at once, rather loudly.

Robinson stood still and sighed.

'But I must send a wire to London in the morning,' I said.

'There's no post office on Robinson. It is a very small island.' He added, since I suppose I looked startled, 'You are safe. I think you will be able to get up tomorrow. Then you shall see what's what.'

He took my empty cup, then sat down in a high wicker chair. The cat jumped on to his lap. 'Bluebell,' he murmured to it. I lay and stared, partly comatose, and it was difficult for me to collect a thought and place it into a sentence. Eventually I said,

'Would you mind telling me, is there a nurse, a woman anywhere about?'

He peered forward as if to compel my attention. 'That

must be a difficulty for you. There is no woman on the island. But it is not difficult for me to nurse you. It will only be for a short while. Besides, it is necessary.' He put the cat off his lap. 'Regard me as a doctor or something like that.'

A man's voice called from the inner house.

'That's one of the other patients,' said Robinson.

'How many . . . the accident. How many?'

'I'll be back soon,' he said.

I thought he showed fatigue as he left my range of vision. Bluebell camelled her back, stalked on to my mattress, curled up, and began to purr.

We were a thousand miles from anywhere. I think the effects of the concussion were still upon me when I got up, the fourth morning after the crash. It was some time before I took in the details of Robinson's establishment, and not till a week later that I began to wonder at his curious isolation.

By that time there was no hope of our immediate rescue. Many of you will remember how the whole of the Atlantic had been notified, how military aircraft and commercial airlines searched for us, and all ships kept a look-out for survivors or portions of the wreck. Meantime, there we were on Robinson, with the wreck and the corpses. The island had been under mist when the first search party came over shortly after the crash. Robinson lit distress signals every night, but when, two nights later, the searchers returned, a torrent of rain had quenched the flares. On both occasions the plane had retreated quickly out of the mist, fearful of our mountain. There was nothing but to wait for the pomegranate boat in August.

My left arm ached in its sling when I rose dizzily from my couch on the floor, but dazed as I was, Robinson sent me immediately to nurse Tom Wells who lay with broken

13

ribs encased in a tight jacket which Robinson had contrived, made of canvas strips bound diagonally from back to front, the layers overlapping each other by two-thirds. Robinson explained the principle of this jacket very carefully before telling me that in any case I mustn't remove it from the patient. My hours of duty were from eight in the morning until three in the afternoon, when Robinson relieved me.

A long thin man, with his head bound in a proper bandage, did night shifts, and I believe Robinson took over from him also, during the night, so that someone was always ready to attend to Tom Wells.

Robinson had introduced me to the tall man; I recollect his naming me 'Miss January', but I did not catch the man's name, although he seemed familiar to me. I asked Robinson several times in those first days, 'Who is the other nurse? What's his name?' but it was a full week before the name had sunk in, Jimmie Waterford. This Jimmie was very friendly to me, as if we were previously acquainted. It was some time before I remembered having met him on the Lisbon plane. The monosyllabic 'Tom Wells', however, stuck in my mind right away.

About this time I became aware of a small lean boy, about nine years old, very brown and large-eyed. I had seen him when I first got up, but did not really notice him for several days. He followed Robinson everywhere. He had certain duties, like fetching small consignments of firewood into the house and making tea. His name was Miguel.

In the mornings Robinson would give me instructions. I followed them with meticulous care, as one dazed and unable to exercise curiosity. Meanwhile Robinson and the tall man would go off together for two or three hours at a time.

Tom Wells, besides being the most seriously injured, was a difficult patient. He moaned or made noises nearly all day, although Robinson gave him injections. He seemed to have grasped our situation and was, in fact, more conscious than I was at that time. I have always been against nurses who won't stand nonsense from their patients, but I found myself becoming snappy and sharp with Tom Wells, as to the manner born. Robinson would smile in his weary manner, when he overheard me telling the man, 'Stop that noise', 'Pull yourself together', 'Drink this', and so on. All this, before I had in any way got my new environment into focus. I knew, with an inhuman indifference, that there had been an accident. I accepted the situation of being simply in a place, that Robinson was in charge, and that I was to look after Tom Wells at certain fixed times.

Exactly a week after the accident, Robinson said to me at breakfast, 'Try to eat as little as you can. Most of our food is tinned, and I had not counted on guests.'

It was only then that I realized I was eating at all. Robinson had produced meals, and I now presumed I had been eating them. I looked at my plate on the round pale-wood table. I had just finished a portion of yellowish beans. Beside my plate was half a hard thick dry biscuit, of a type which I now recalled having dipped into strong warm tea during the past few days.

After that, I noticed the place more closely. When I began that day to act independently of Robinson, he seemed relieved. It was two days later that he gave me the exercise book for my journal.

I wanted to be at home again, giggling with Agnes and Julia when they came to tea on cold afternoons. Giggling over childhood anecdotes was the main thing with my sisters, and how, afterwards, I would wonder at my own childishness!

And yet, at those moments, I enjoyed the silly sessions. There had been a time, after my elopement as a schoolgirl, the birth of my son, and my widowhood that same year, when I was estranged from my sisters. From Agnes, because she was the eldest: lumpy, unmarried, and resenting my adventure. Agnes kept house for our grandmother. When Grandmother died, Agnes married the doctor; she married after all. We became friends, up to the point where it is possible to be friends with Agnes, who eats noisily, for one thing.

My younger sister, Julia, was still at school when I ran away from it to marry. Six months later my husband was dead. I tried to take an interest in Julia, with her tall prettiness. But she was considered a loose girl; I thought so too. 'It's nothing but men, men, men, with Julia,' I said once to Agnes.

'Oh, shut up,' said Agnes.

Years later, Julia married a bookie. They were married in a register office. I was not invited. I saw the bookie at Grandmother's funeral; I mistook him for the undertaker at first.

'I mistook him for the undertaker,' I whispered to Agnes.

'Oh, shut up,' said Agnes. She did not tell me then that she planned to marry the doctor within a month.

After that, when we began to be reconciled, Julia and Agnes would come to tea with me, though I rarely visited them. Agnes lived at Chiswick and Julia at Wimbledon, and it is a bother to get to those places from Chelsea. We soon found the only common ground between us – our childhood. We would giggle till about six o'clock when my son Brian would come in, rosy-cheeked from his school games. My sisters would never leave without seeing him. I fancied they envied me Brian, for the years went on and both were childless.

When I had run away as a schoolgirl, and Brian was born, Agnes had shown no interest in the child. Her curiosity was in my direction. 'You're far too young for this sort of caper,' she said from her privileged position as a visitor in a nursing-home – she perpendicular, I horizontal. 'I thought you were supposed to have brains,' she said.

But when they saw Brian in later years, both my sisters were, I think, surprised at his lack of blight; they had somehow expected the child of such a young girl to grow up peculiar.

'Goodness,' said Julia after the funeral, 'look at January's boy. Isn't he a real *boy*!'

But they had yet to discover Brian's extraordinary social skill, for that side of his personality had already, in his middle teens, advanced beyond his age.

'Goodness,' said Julia, 'hasn't he got *charm*!'

I often wondered if Agnes and Julia really came to visit Brian, not me; trailing all that way from Chiswick and Wimbledon on cold afternoons. Even during the first phase of my religious conversion, when I took to lecturing my sisters, they continued to come.

Journal, May 20, 1954 – The area of Robinson is only a little over 84 square miles, if you can call them square that run in such strange directions. Robinson bought the island fifteen years ago from a Portuguese and settled here after the war. Its former name was Ferreira. Robinson showed me a map. If you hold it east-upmost it resembles a human shape. There are several peninsulas which Robinson calls the North Arm and the South Arm of the island, the North Leg and the West Leg. Robinson's house is on a plateau nearly a thousand feet above the sea. It is a volcanic mountain, only cinders and lava at the top, but he says the descent passes through the range of known climates. R. once sprained his ankle up there, when he tripped on a patch of ling. In July the upper third of the mountain is covered with flowering thyme. I have these facts from Robinson. He has given me this notebook. He said, 'Keep to facts, that will be the healthiest course.' I am always tired.

Now, as I look at the crinkled page of my first journal entry, I recall that it was Robinson's idea to write very small, to make no paragraphs, to save the paper. Even so, the exercise book did not last out my time on the island; I had later to use some loose writing paper which I found on Robinson's desk.

I recall that Robinson had advised more than once, 'Stick to facts.' He had advised strongly against gazing at the sea in the hope of a boat or at the sky for a plane – a depressing habit, he said. I could scarcely keep my eyes from the sea and sky in those first weeks, although the boat which would bring Robinson's provisions and take away his pomegranates was not due at the south coast until the second week of August. I had been pressing Robinson about the possibility of constructing a radio transmitter. He said there were no means. I thought as I wrote my first journal, 'By now Brian will believe me to be dead.' But I did not write this down, as I did not know it for a fact.

Chapter 2

ROBINSON's house was an early nineteenth-century building in an earlier Spanish style. It was a stone bungalow set on a wide natural terrace of the mountain. Around it ran a low wall, and over this, from my room, I could see the blue and green lake on mornings when there was no mist. I did not go beyond the great arched wrought-iron gates in the first two weeks. Instead, when my confusion had dissipated, and when I had time off from nursing Tom Wells, I wandered in the small neglected garden or sat in the neglected patio, stroking my injured shoulder and watching the fountain that did not play.

Most of the rooms had been out of use, apparently for some months. I swept them out. Three rooms and the big stone kitchen served as Robinson's living quarters. Miguel slept in a small room amongst a great amount of fishing equipment. The other rooms were curiously furnished, each one with three floor-beds, mere pallets stuffed with a silky material made out of a local fern, a wicker chair and a polished wood table. Each one had a carved crucifix on the wall. As soon as I had my wits more alert I questioned Robinson about these rooms.

'Who sleeps there, usually?'

'The pomegranate men,' he answered. 'They are plantation workers who arrive every August by the boat. They remain for three or four weeks working on the pomegranate orchard up at the Headlands and gathering in the fruit, while the boat does business at the Canaries and the west coast of Africa.'

'And the rest of the year you live alone on the island?'

'Yes.'

'With Miguel,' I added, pumping him for a clue about the boy.

'Miguel has been with me five years. He is to go to school later this year, and then I will be alone with myself again.'

Certainly I did inquire: 'Whose child is Miguel?'

'You do like to get everything straight,' Robinson said mysteriously.

I was silent then. I was not so concussed that I failed to gather that Robinson was leading me on in some way to express my suspicions. It then flashed upon me that Miguel was not, as in fact I had suspected, Robinson's own child, probably illegitimate.

'Quite a mystery, isn't it?' said Robinson, quite eager for me to agree.

'I see no mystery. I can guess his origin,' I said, meantime wondering what I myself meant, quite.

'What is it then? What's your guess?'

'He's an orphan of one of the pomegranate men who died, and you've adopted him,' I said for some reason.

Robinson said: 'You must have heard it from Waterford.'

'I've never been to Waterford.'

'Jimmie Waterford,' he said. 'The tall fair man who was on the plane with you. He must have told you about my adopting Miguel. He knows a little of my affairs.' He seemed to accuse me as he spoke.

'No,' I said, 'it was a guess. I thought it likely.'

He seemed relieved. 'You know,' he said, 'I expected you to place the paternity on me.'

'No, that would not be likely,' I said.

'Good gracious me,' said Robinson, looking at me. 'Women,' he said, 'do come out with things.'

Journal, Sunday, 23rd May – This is the end of our second week on Robinson. My shoulder hurts. I suppose it will need electrical treatment when I get home, if ever. I am sitting in the doorway of my room. J[immie] W[aterford] has just returned, and is milking the goat. Robinson is absent. I know now where they have been in the day-time while I have been nursing Tom Wells. First they buried the dead. Next they started examining the wreck, and they are now salvaging from it. Miguel fishes in the stream all morning. Robinson has a list of the dead. There are twenty-six items, and only four names of which he is certain. The others are described by anything which happened to be attached to the corpse, such as a metal watch-band dangling, I suppose, on the charred wrist, a ring on a finger-bone, or a lucky charm worn under the shirt. Robinson has been very efficient. I have seen the list. I am free to walk about on the island now that the dead are buried. Jimmie is singing as he milks the goat, I think a Dutch song. He is partly Dutch, his name was not always Waterford. I remember, now, that I met him on the plane before we crashed. His pronunciation of English is quite good, and his vocabulary most unusual. I think R. is worried about Jimmie, in a personal way, as if he were not a stranger. Jimmie looks slightly like Robinson, about the nose. This is a suspicion. Robinson advised, stick to facts, write facts. All right, there is the fact about Tom Wells, his behaviour to me this morning. I shall have to complain to Robinson.

On that morning I had carried to Tom Wells at noon a bowl of cream of tomato soup which we had opened for him. It was set on a tray with some of our hard, thick biscuits. I balanced it in my right hand, my left still being in its sling.

Tom Wells was propped up; for the past week his health had been improving. As I approached his bed, which was a real bed, not, like mine, a mattress on the floor, he said, 'Have they all been interred?'

'Yes.'

He put out his hand and touched me.

'You're a nice piece of homework,' he said.

I think I could have saved the soup. Really, I do not know, maybe I deliberately let go of the tray. The soup tipped over him, down the front of his shirt and over the sheets, like blood in a Technicolor film.

Leaving him in this plight I returned to the kitchen, where Robinson was carving a duck-like bird which he had roasted. Jimmie had his back to the door, and when I entered he was speaking rapidly and softly in his Dutch language. Robinson saw me and said to Jimmie in an open voice:

'Miss January is here.'

The scene with Tom Wells had unnerved me.

'My name is not *Miss* January. I am Mrs Marlow.'

'Well, well,' said Robinson.

I said, 'I have spilt the soup over Tom Wells.'

Robinson went out, returning presently for another bowl of soup. I sat at the kitchen table and ate the meal, staring glumly.

Jimmie Waterford, with his long arms, reached in front of me for the bread. His blond head was out of bandages now.

When Robinson joined us Jimmie addressed me:

'Ha!' he said. 'No man is an island.'

'Some are,' I said. 'Their only ground of meeting is concealed under the sea. If words mean anything, and islands exist, then some people are islands.'

'That's a point,' said Robinson.

'Is so,' said Jimmie, 'mayhaps.'

That afternoon I wrote the journal entry and in the evening I said to Robinson,

'You must make other arrangements about Wells. I won't nurse him.'

'I am not obliged to make any arrangements for anyone,' he said. 'Have sense,' he added, mimicking Jimmie who used often to say, 'Have sense.'

'I will not be left alone with that man in this house.'

'Be reasonable,' said Robinson.

'You must speak to him,' I said. 'Warn him. Threaten.'

'I shall say you wear a knife in your stocking.'

Of course I had no stockings. I was lucky to have legs.

'Listen to the frogs,' I said, for I had calmed down, and the frogs were howling among the rushes in the mountain lake.

'How long have you been married?'

'I'm a widow,' I said, 'and a journalist' – I thought this was understating the case, but it provided an approximate category to poet, critic, and general articulator of ideas. Now that my head was clear I was a little tired of hearing Robinson's advice, 'Keep up your journal. Stick to facts. Describe the scenery', as if, in the normal way, I could not put words together.

Robinson remarked, 'Those are two conditions of life which make for resourcefulness. You can handle Wells yourself. Try to hide your dislike of him.'

'Oh, I've nothing against him, apart from his conduct this morning.'

'Why, of course you have,' said Robinson.

It occurred to me that Robinson resembled, in appearance, my brother-in-law, Ian Brodie, the doctor whom Agnes had married. It was not a strong resemblance – a matter only of the shape of the head, but I wished that it did not exist, seeing that I should have to live with Robinson till August.

Chapter 3

'HELP yourself to any of my books,' Robinson said.

Now, he had a large library behind glass bookcases. I should not, myself, put books behind glass. Here at home the books are not neat. Robinson's library was well bound and groomed. I observed that some were uncut first editions. I am addicted to a form of snobbery which will hardly keep a first edition on its shelves. To think of a man keeping uncut first editions on an island gave me a snobbish sort of amusement.

Although my married life had lasted only six months, my husband had conditioned many of my tastes. When I ran away from school to marry him he was fifty-eight, a Classics professor whose mother was connected by marriage to my grandmother. Until he met me he had led a retired life. It was a shock to me to discover he had married me for a bet. Sometimes, when I wondered how it would have been had he lived, and I came to realize how old he would have been – seventy-four at the time of my stay on the island, I shuddered, thinking absurdly of the wrinkled hands of old men. In spite of that, and although my tastes did no longer exactly incline to the scholarly type of man, such as I had married, my taste in books was largely a perpetuation of his. Inside the cover of all Robinson's books was a bookplate marked with the words:

Ex Libris

Miles Mary Robinson

below which was a fairly dreadful woodcut representing a book open on a table lectern, a quill pen, and an old-fashioned lamp on the table. Beneath this, in gothic lettering, was the motto *Nunquam minus solus quam cum solus.*

Jimmie Waterford came to find me, very shortly after the incident with Tom Wells and the soup. I was teaching the cat to play ping-pong in a corner of the patio, while brown Miguel looked on, silent and very contemptuous of this occupation.

'One thing,' said Jimmie, 'I tell.'

'Hallo, Jimmie,' I said.

Jimmie squatted down and I put the ping-pong ball in my pocket for the next lesson.

'Please to go make tea for Mr Tom Wells,' he said to Miguel.

I realized he wanted to talk to me privately, and so I settled myself beside him.

'Is this,' he said. 'To tell you Robinson isn't man for the ladies. I am not a stranger to Robinson.'

I knew already that he was familiar with Robinson. And there was the likeness about the nose which now caused me to think they might be related.

I had taken rather a liking to Jimmie on the Lisbon plane. This was partly because of his peculiar idiom of English speech which I later learned had been acquired, first from a Swiss uncle, using Shakespeare and some seventeenth-century poets as textbooks, and Fowler's *Modern English Usage* as a guide, and secondly from contact with Allied forces during the war. And, on the plane, I had taken to Jimmie also because of his seeming unpremeditation in talking to me in the first place.

'Is bad weather to fly.'

'Now, is it?' I said.

'You like a drink? Lo!'

He screwed the cap off his leather and silver flask, and removed the flat cup from its base.

'I don't think so, thanks,' I said by way of form.

'You take the cup, I swig from the vessel,' he said, handing me the cup half-filled with brandy.

Just then a member of the crew with his head bent and brown chin sunk into his neck walked rapidly aft. Within a few seconds he walked quickly back again and disappeared from sight. That was the first and last I saw of the crew of our plane. In the meantime Jimmie was telling me,

'I think I want my head examined. Mayhaps you think I come on a holiday. Oh no, oh no. Do you make holiday?'

'No, business,' I said. 'Lovely brandy,' I said, 'it makes me feel more normal.'

There were clouds molten in the setting sun beneath us and we were going into cloud, climb as we might.

'I think you are not a business woman,' said Jimmie, taking a pull from his flask.

'Thanks,' I said.

'Is a compliment,' Jimmie pointed out.

'I see,' I said amiably. 'Thanks.'

'I furnish you with a little more hooch.'

'No, thanks. I've had enough. It was nice.'

None the less, he poured some more brandy into my cup which I sipped appreciatively. I find that, when travelling abroad alone, it is wise and actually discreet to take up with one well-chosen man on the journey. Otherwise, one is likely to be approached by numerous chance pesterers all along the line. One must, of course, discriminate, but it is a thing one learns by experience, how to know the sort of man who is not likely to press for future commitments. I felt I was lucky to meet with Jimmie. In fact, I had more or less picked on him at the airport, out of a need for protection from a broad-faced English commercial man with a loud voice and a lot of luggage who had been looking much my way. There were also a couple of Spaniards, who when I failed to recognize their separate salutations, had teamed up with each other.

While I sipped Jimmie's brandy, I heard the broad-faced Englishman's voice from several yards to the fore, engaged in conversation with an American couple.

'Just let me open the brief-case,' he was saying. 'I'll show you the article. I tell you, the pattern dates back to the time of the Druids.' He fished into his case and produced a circular badge of white metal about three inches in diameter. I could not make out the interior design but it looked like a gnome sitting on a bar within the circle.

'It's infallible, I can tell you,' said the Englishman. 'It brings the owner *the* most incredible luck. You see, the shape and pattern is a replica to an nth, an *nth* of an inch, of an ancient Druid charm discovered on the moors of Devonshire, England, only fifty-seven years ago. It is a magic charm. *How* it works, or why, I don't pretend to know. But it works.'

'Well, now,' said the American lady.

'Well, now,' said her husband.

'We unloaded five hundred thousand the last half of last year to New Zealand alone,' said the Englishman.

'Well, now.'

'If you ask me,' Jimmie said softly to me, 'for my part I imagine perchance he wants his head examined.'

I sipped the brandy and nodded agreeably.

'Hey, there,' said the Englishman so that his voice carried all up the saloon, and the Americans looked abashed. 'I've been ringing for you, my dear boy,' he said, as the suntanned steward appeared. 'I fancy a whisky – and what about my friends here?'

'Lemon squash,' said the American lady.

'Tonic,' said her husband.

'You need something stronger than that. You stopping at Santa Maria? It's damp there, I can tell you.'

'Well, now,' said the American lady. 'A squash.'

'Whisky and tonic,' said her husband.

'Going home to the States?'

'Well, now, Bermuda first,' said the American lady, her eyes glued to the magic charm which the Englishman was holding between finger and thumb.

Jimmie remarked to me, 'That man is holding converse in a loud key.'

'I did see this chappie at the airport,' said Jimmie, 'and in the moment I behold him I perceive he is not a superior type of bugger. I say to myself, Lo! this one is not a gentleman.'

'Really?' I said.

'I have the instinct for the gentlemen,' said Jimmie, 'as likewise for the ladies.'

I thought, 'He is a most amusing companion', and meanwhile the plane began to bump through the weather to the Azores. Jimmie's face was long and fine; his nose turned up slightly at the bridge giving him a humorous expression; his hair was very light; I judged his age to be in the early thirties.

'You cross the Atlantic Ocean?' he said.

'I'm stopping at the Azores.'

'Myself likewise. And in the long run,' he said, 'I proceed southward by the sea to another island.'

'Which island is that? I'm rather interested in islands.'

'Is not on the map. Is too small.'

The man with the lucky charms was asking his friends, 'You know your future?'

'Pardon?' said the American lady.

'The magazine *Your Future*?'

'Well, now, I don't.'

'I own it *and* I run it,' said the man.

I noticed that the sun had set.

· · · · ·

When, at the end of my second week on Robinson, I began to recognize Jimmie, I was immensely cheered up by the memory of our conversation on the plane. The tall fair man with his head in bandages regained in my eyes the shape and status of my amusing travelling companion.

When he squatted on the patio repeating, 'Robinson is not man for the ladies. I know Robinson from the past', I was not at all surprised. I had already noticed that he was familiar with Robinson, and had gathered that, in fact, Robinson had been that ultimate destination to which he had referred in the plane.

'Robinson is not man for the ladies.'

That, too, I knew already. There is easily discernible in some men a certain indifference, not to women precisely but to the feminine element in women, which might be interpreted in a number of ways. In Robinson I had detected something more than indifference: a kind of armed neutrality. So much for his attitude to me. And I thought it likely that he could be positively hostile to the idea of women in general.

'Look here,' I said to Jimmie, 'I wasn't born yesterday.'

'Is so?' said Jimmie gallantly.

'And in any case,' I said, 'Robinson is not my style.'

'Do not become rattled,' said Jimmie, 'in consequence of what I say.'

'You can tell Robinson from me –'

'Ah me!' said Jimmie, 'I am not messenger from Robinson. I tell you this from my own heart.'

That put a different complexion on things. I was quite charmed by Jimmie. He appealed to a quality in my mind which I considered the most advanced I possessed, and which was also slightly masculine.

'You like this?' said Jimmie.

He held out to me a little shining lipstick case. I took it and opened it. The lipstick inside was almost unused, but not quite. There was a little blunt smear at the end. Suddenly I threw it with a clink into the dry fountain.

'It is salvage,' I said. I was not only repelled by the idea of using a dead woman's lipstick, I was furious at Jimmie's implication that I might entertain a romantic interest in Robinson.

'Is true,' he said.

Having buried the dead, they had been gathering from the environs of the burnt-out plane everything that remained a recognizable object. It was surprising, the sort of things they had picked up several hundred yards from the wreckage. Among them were my reading glasses intact in their case, with my name and address in Chelsea on the inside. I had said, when Robinson handed them to me,

'I'd rather have my make-up case. I can read without the glasses.'

'Can't you read without the make-up?'

'I don't feel quite myself without make-up.' This was true. And I was not made any happier by the condition of my dress and coat, though I had patched them up since the accident.

And so, when Jimmie offered me this gruesome lipstick, I felt sure that Robinson had repeated my complaint. I darkly discerned they had been discussing me considerably as a female problem. I left Jimmie sitting on the patio, and thinking how I must keep my end up, I helped myself to a couple of Robinson's cigarettes above my allotted ration. I was the only other smoker besides Robinson on the island, and he had generously, though with an air of resignation, agreed to share with me, strictly fifty-fifty, his total supply for the duration of our stay. This gave us nine cigarettes a day each. As a result of his discussing me with Jimmie, and the incident of the lipstick, I had eleven cigarettes that day, while Robinson had only seven. I felt that this course was preferable to nurturing a grudge.

Chapter 4

AT the end of the third week Tom Wells was able to get up. He still wore the canvas contrivance in which Robinson had, with good success, encased his broken ribs which seemed to be knitting together nicely. This left me free from my nursing duties, and all the afternoons were my own. And now that the dead were buried I was free to wander about the island.

'If you're going for a walk,' said Robinson, 'take this raincoat. The weather is a woman in this island.' It was my first excursion, a sunny day, the sixth of June, the Feast of Pentecost.

I already had one arm in the garment when I peeled it off and threw it on the ground as if it were teeming with maggots. The violent action hurt my left arm which was just out of its sling.

'It is salvage,' I said.

Robinson sighed and picked it up. 'Borrow mine,' he said.

Robinson's waterproof was not much too big for me. For my first walk, he advised the path down the mountain to the south coast of the island, along the white beach, and returning by a second mountain path which was visible from the villa on clear days. Robinson pointed out the whole route from his gateway, for there was no mist.

The descent did not start immediately from Robinson's villa. The house was built on a flat shoulder wide enough to contain the blue and green lake and a patch of ground the size of a field which was visible from the patio. Robinson had planted this field with mustard which was now in bloom so that I was almost dazzled by its shimmering yellow. Placed so near the lake, the field was a startling

31

sight. 'I planted mustard for the effect,' he said. Apart from the pomegranates, which he cultivated on an eastern part of the island as a business, he did not grow any of his own food. No runner beans, potatoes, onions, spinach, rhubarb, no tomato frames nor currant bushes, nor peaches and plums. A large storehouse behind the house held his quantities of tinned supplies and grain. I thought this odd, since the ground on the plateau surrounding the villa was fertile and the sun blazing hot, and the mists gentle and frequent.

This was the first day since the accident that I had been alone with myself. I planned eventually to explore the whole island. Robinson had told us of a lava-landscape on the other side of the mountain which, he said, was like moon scenery. There was also an active crater. This excited me. But Robinson warned me against wandering further than the south beach on this my first excursion.

The gradient was irregular, gentle and steep by turns. At one point I had to scramble down over old lava flows. Here I took my foothold on tough beds of thyme and ling about four inches high, and eventually came to a grassy woodland and a clump of blue gum trees which, from Robinson's villa, had looked like dwarf vegetation.

I must say that throughout my stay on the island I was more observant of my surroundings than I had ever been before, or have been since. I had often, previously, been accustomed to topographical observations, but that had been according to rule, deliberate. Now, without any effort of will, my eye recorded the territory, as if my eyes were an independent and aboriginal body, taking precautions against unknown eventualities. Instinctively I looked for routes of escape, positions of concealment, protective rocks; instinctively I looked for edible vegetation. In fact, I must have been afraid. And whereas, on my previous travels, I had been scenery and landscape-minded, had been botanically inclined, had been geologically enchanted, had known the luxury of anthropological speculations, I found myself now noting the practical shelter to be obtained from small craters and gulches and lava caverns. Fissures, cracks and holes attracted me for their contents of nettles and fungus, possibly edible. One could keep a fire alight more easily at a level above the mist-belt; one could, if necessary, survive, and bed down on bracken from these lower woodlands. Fresh-water streams were frequent. One night spent on the sphagnum moors of the cloud-belt would be fatal. On the other side of the mountain, where Robinson used to disappear for several hours on end, there was plenty of game, as I knew from his occasional reappearance with woodcock, partridge and sometimes snipe; or sometimes he brought back a rabbit. I now wished I had learned to use a gun. I had been told of a fresh-water stream from which Miguel was clever at getting trout. I wondered in what part of the island this stream could be. And then I wondered what all the panic was about. I had apparently nothing to fear.

As I climbed down the pathway among the last of the lava rocks to the coast I saw Miguel approaching along the beach. I waved. He saw me, but did not respond. Miguel was not hostile exactly, but he was difficult to please. I think in those first four weeks he was jealous of our having appeared out of the skies and drawn off all Robinson's attention.

He had spent the greater part of his childhood with Robinson, with whom he spoke good English. His mother having died in his infancy, the father had attached himself to a trading boat and become one of Robinson's pomegranate men. Miguel had always accompanied his father on his working periods on Robinson, and, when the father had died, Robinson adopted the child. Robinson spoke often of Miguel's forthcoming departure for school in Lisbon, as if it were a great but inevitable misfortune. He had not yet fixed on any particular school, so strong was his disinclination to part with Miguel.

Of course I had attempted to strike up a friendship with Miguel but so far there was nothing doing. Jimmie had also failed in this respect. A sort of competition had developed between us for the child's attention, let alone affection. Tom Wells, who was only now risen from his sick-bed, had so far been too taken up with his own discomfort to notice him, but Jimmie and I had been disconcerted to find, on Tom Wells's first afternoon out of bed, when he had been sat up with blankets on the patio, that Miguel had hung shyly round the man, who did not attempt to encourage the child, particularly. The next day, Robinson, with an air of omnipotent indulgence, brought to Tom Wells his own brief-case which had happened to be among the salvage – it having presumably been clutched in Wells's hands at the time of his projection from the plane. As Tom Wells seized on this with delight and began to examine the contents, Miguel had approached without further hesitation, and thrust his brown hand into the interior.

'Let me see,' he said, snuggling up to Wells, 'what you've got there.'

He was overjoyed when Tom Wells produced one of his sample Druid emblems.

Jimmie and I were quite put out. My attempts to teach the cat Bluebell to play ping-pong were partly inspired by a desire to impress Miguel. He seemed to think it was an unworthy idea. Jimmie, who had been suffering from delayed shock, although his physical injuries had been slight, went so far as to attempt a cart-wheel on the patio, and suffered a nasty nose-bleed as a result. Miguel was indifferent. I fetched the great cold key from the kitchen and put it down Jimmie's back. Miguel watched uppishly and without comment. 'That youngster doesn't even bloody laugh at my great sorrow,' said Jimmie, dabbing his nose.

And so I was not surprised when Miguel did not wave back to me from the beach, although I saw him look up. He had certainly seen me. I decided to amble along the beach towards him. The sand was extremely fine, and less white than it had looked from a distance against the black lava rocks. Up against the cliffs some pink star-shaped flowers were opening out of the very sand. A few yards away from where the cliff path joined the beach, the ribs of a small sailing vessel lay half-buried, and farther along was the wreck of an old clipper, its leonine figurehead still intact and pointing skyward. I cleared a space among the weed on the mouldering forepart and sat there to rest, leaning on the bowsprit and rubbing my painful left arm.

When he saw me sitting there, Miguel stopped self-consciously. He lifted a pebble and threw it into the curling sea. At this coast the sea was two miles deep and the currents were dangerous. Robinson had warned us not to bathe in the sea, for even where the currents were safe the sharks were not. The blue-green lake was the island bathing-pool.

From the map of Robinson which he had shown me I knew that this stretch of beach lay in the small of the back. I could not help thinking of the island in this anatomical way, because of Robinson's constant references to the Arms and Legs.

Miguel continued to throw pebbles, and I watched the sea, in case he should be embarrassed by my watching him. There was a special fascination about the sea surrounding Robinson, stretching for a thousand miles to the nearest post office. It was only a few seconds later that I realized Miguel had stopped chucking pebbles, and I fancied he must be approaching. I looked along the beach but could see no sign of him, although I had a view of the whole stretch. A small strip of vegetation grew against the black cliffs, but this was too low to hide Miguel unless he lay flat.

I decided he must be lying flat, and set off along the beach, examining the base of the cliffs very closely. I reached the end of the beach, where the black rock rose sheer out of the sea, without having found any trace of Miguel. I was bewildered, then frightened. I could see no place where he could be concealed except the sea. I scanned the sea fearfully, hoping I should not see a head bobbing far out of my reach, but I saw nothing but the waves chopping with the undercurrents, which might have concealed anything. I did not really think he could have jumped into the sea in the few moments that my eyes had been turned from him. I did not really think he would be so foolish. I was sure Miguel was somewhere safe but I was disturbed by having no reason for this certainty. For a moment I thought perhaps they had never existed, that Robinson and his household were a dead woman's dream, that I was indeed dead as my family believed and the newspapers had by now reported. In view of these ideas, I thought the most necessary course of action was to return to Robinson's house by the shortest route and report the disappearance of Miguel.

The quickest route led from the end of the beach where I now stood, although it was not exactly the shortest. It zig-zagged up the mountain, a gentler gradient than that of the path I had used on my downward journey. I had been tacking up this path for twenty minutes when I came upon a derelict croft-house and watermill on a small plateau overhanging a stream which trickled down a small ravine. It now struck me that Robinson's predecessors, hermits though they might be, had made efforts to cultivate every green spot on the island. Later, when I saw the rich pasture-lands of the West Leg and South Arm, I felt a sort of outrage that their work was falling to waste. I saw by the croft-house a number of mango trees still bearing fruit, but they were bedraggled and untended. It was from here that

Robinson must have gathered the poor specimens of mango which we ate for breakfast. I did not suppose the trees would bear much longer.

Many times, during my climb, I had turned to scan the beach below and the surrounding mountain scrub for some sign of Miguel. I began to worry seriously, mainly because I had every obvious reason to worry. When I came up to the deserted croft I took a last look round, for above this plateau the cloud-belt was forming as it usually did in the late afternoon, and this made it impossible to see the coast-line from where I stood.

I decided to rest from my climb for ten minutes on this plateau, and I ambled about, walking round the cottage, looking through the gaping windows. I tried the door. It was open. I entered, and saw Miguel by the crumbling hearth laying twigs for a fire. He had a can of water and a tin of coffee.

'Hallo,' I said. 'How did you get here?'

He looked pleased with this question, and so, to please him more, I said,

'I saw you on the beach. I looked away for a moment, and when I looked again you were gone.'

He even laughed at this.

'How did you do it?' I said. If he had climbed the mountain I must have seen him. But he must have climbed the mountain and I did not see him.

'There's a secret cave,' said Miguel, 'with a tunnel.'

'Where? I should like to see it.'

He shook his head.

'Does Robinson know the secret cave?'

'Yes. But he won't show it.'

He handed me a tin mug of his hot black coffee brew.

'Robinson won't show you the caves. He only shows me.'

'Oh, is there more than one?'

He did not answer, having already let slip too much.

'This is lovely stuff,' I said, and lest I should seem patronizing, I added, 'but it needs some sugar.'

He fished into the inside pocket of his lumber jacket and brought out a paper screw of sugar. This he opened and emptied into my mug, stirring it with a twig. We sat on the hearthstone and sipped. Meantime I was wishing I was at home.

'I'm off now,' said Miguel.

'I'm coming too,' I said.

'No, you wait a short time.'

I thought he wanted to go to some other secret caves and didn't want me to discover the way, so I said,

'All right. Let's say about ten minutes. Will that do?'

'Well,' he said, 'you wait till it stops raining.'

I noticed that it was raining, not very heavily.

'Oh, is that all?' I said. 'Well, I don't mind the rain.'

'Robinson's raincoat will get wet,' the boy pointed out.

I could not deny it. I waited till the shower was over, then emerged to catch sight of Miguel making his nimble way home through the thicket above me.

Chapter 5

'I wish,' said Jimmie, 'I stay at home. I commence to think I want my head examined for making this dangerous journey.'

'Same here,' I said, without really meaning it.

I did wish to go home, but not that I had never come away. If I had stayed at home, there might have been a fire in the house, or I might have been run over, or murdered, or have committed a mortal sin. There is no absolute method of judging whether one course of action is less dangerous than another.

'Same here,' I said, simply to convey agreement that our situation might be better than it was.

We had brought a picnic and were settled on the banks of the blue and green lake. In front of us was a lumpy patch of goat meadow leaning down towards the cliff, and below, since there was no mist, was the sea. To our right was the vivid yellow mustard field. The effect was fairly Arcadian, if only one could relax and enjoy it.

'Why did you come?' I said. I was curious to know where Jimmie had come from, why he had taken the Lisbon plane to the Azores with the purpose of finding his way to Robinson, how long he had known Robinson, and at the same time was irritated by this curiosity of mine which did so indicate that these people were becoming part of my world. I had rather regarded them as travelling companions – as one might take up with a man on a plane. I like to be in a position to choose, I like to be in control of my relationships with people.

On the sixth of June I had written in my journal:

39

I feel that we were all unwelcome on the island. The emergency is over. Tom Wells is now able to get about. I am beginning to use my left arm. Jimmie, who received only a small cut in the head, and in fact had not even lost consciousness at the time of the crash, is suffering from nerves. Robinson seems rather irritated by all of us.

'Why did you come?' I said to Jimmie.

'Is Robinson's vast properties,' he replied. 'Robinson's family beseech me, "Go and bring back Robinson to his birthright. Begone, we shall foot the bill." Thus, I came. But is first I should reside at marvellous Azores and next is pleasant ocean voyage to the island of Robinson which I envisage, and to behold my kinsman old Robinson. Mayhaps a month I should reside here, or two. I should say, "Robinson, return!" He should say, "Not me, chum." I should say to him, "Is properties, Robinson. The old uncle has died and, behold, the properties fall to neglect." Robinson should reply, "So what?" and I should say, "Who is to administer these great estates?" He should tell me, "Not me, chum. Is all yours." And I figure, six months should elapse before I return my steps towards the family of Robinson to reveal to them I fail in my great mission. As I have planned, I should say to them, "I fail." They say to me, "Alas." They pay the bill. So I have had six months' merry voyaging and they should pay up. Whereafter they should say, "Now who shall administer these properties?" I say, "Robinson desires this post to me." But,' said Jimmie, 'this destiny has not come to pass. Is fizzle out, and I fall from the sky. I languish.'

'I don't see,' I said, 'how your plans are changed at all. You can still return within six months and take over Robinson's affairs for him.'

'All is changed,' said Jimmie, 'since I am cast from the heavens. Is numerous dead. Robinson is cross. I lose my nerves. Robinson takes no care for the honour of his family.'

I began to reflect on Robinson's lordly estates.

'Where are these properties?' I inquired.

'In Tangier,' said Jimmie.

'Do his family live in Tangier?'

'No, in Gibraltar. They possess abundant cash. I am but the poor kinsman.'

'What sort of lands do they possess in Tangier?'

'Is not lands. Is motor-scooters. Is vast import business. For my part, I tell you, I should have been fine and dandy a managing director. But I lose my nerves.'

'Never mind,' I said. 'They will come back.'

'Is multitudinous prospects for motor-scooters in the north of Africa. In the course of time I should create many factories. But all is lost. In point of fact I consider how I want my head examined.'

'Perhaps in any case Robinson will return to his family.'

'Nevermore,' said Jimmie. 'I am acquainted with Robinson from the days of my youth, and is for cert he chuck the world.'

To teach a cat to play ping-pong you have first to win the confidence and approval of the cat. Bluebell was the second cat I had undertaken to teach; I found her more amenable than the first, which had been a male.

Ping-pong with a cat is a simplified and more individualistic form of the proper game. You play it close to the ground, and you imagine the net.

Gaining a cat's confidence is different from gaining the confidence of any other animal. Food is not the simple answer. You have to be prepared to play with it for as long as two hours on end. To gain the initial interest of a cat, I always place a piece of paper over my head and face and utter miaows and other cat noises. This is irresistible to most cats, who come nosing up to see what is going on behind the paper. The next phase involves soft whispering alternately with the whistling of high-pitched tunes.

I thought *Bluebells of Scotland* would be appropriate to Bluebell. She was enchanted. It made her purr and rise on her hind legs to paw my shoulder as I crouched on the patio whistling to her in the early afternoons.

After that I began daily to play with her, sometimes throwing the ping-pong ball in the air. She often leapt beautifully and caught it in her forepaws. By the second week in June I had so far won her confidence and approval as to be able to make fierce growling noises at her. She liked these very much, and would crouch menacingly before me, springing suddenly at me in a mock attack. Sometimes I would stalk her, one slow step after another, bent double, and with glaring eyes. She loved this wildly, making flying leaps at my downthrust head.

'You'll get a nasty scratch one day,' said Robinson.

'Oh, I understand cats,' I said.

'She understands cats,' said Jimmie unnecessarily.

Robinson walked away.

Having worked round Bluebell to a stage where she would let me do nearly anything with her and play rough-house as I pleased, I got an old carton out of Robinson's storehouse and set it on end against the patio wall. Bluebell immediately sat herself inside this little three-walled house. Then the first ping-pong lesson began. I knelt down two yards away from her and placed the ball in front of me. She crouched in readiness as if it were an ordinary ball game. With my middle finger and thumb I pinged the ball into Bluebell's box. It bounced against the walls. The cat sprang at it and batted it back. I sent it over again to Bluebell. This time she caught it in her forepaws and curled up on the ground, biting it and kicking it with her silver hind pads. However, for a first lesson her style was not bad. Within a week Bluebell had got the ping-pong idea. Four

times out of ten she would send the ball back to me, sometimes batting it with her hind leg most comically, so that
even Miguel had to laugh. On the other occasions she would
appropriate the ball for herself, either dribbling it right
across the patio, or patting it under her body and then sitting on it. Sometimes she would pat the ball only a little
way in front of her, waiting for me, with her huge green
eyes, to come and retrieve it.

The cat quickly discovered that the setting up of her
carton on the patio was the start of the ping-pong game,
and she was always waiting for me at that spot after lunch.
She was an encouraging pupil, an enthusiast. One day when
she was doing particularly well, and I was encouraging her
with my lion growl to her great excitement, I heard Robinson's voice from the back of the house.

'Bluebell! Pussy-puss Bluebell. Nice puss. Come on!'

Her ear twitched very slightly in response, but she was
at the ball and patting it over to me, it seemed in one
movement. I cracked it back, and she forth again.

'Bluebell! – Where's the cat?' said Robinson, appearing
on the patio just as I was growling more. 'There's a mouse
in the storehouse. Do you *mind*?' he said to me.

The cat had her eyes on my hand which held the ball.
I picked her up and handed her to Robinson. Bluebell
struggled to free herself and go for the ball. I thought this
funny and giggled accordingly. But Bluebell was borne reluctant away by solemn Robinson, with Miguel following
like a righteous little retainer.

Jimmie grinned. Something about Jimmie's grin and
Robinson's bearing embarrassed me. I began to wonder
if Robinson felt intensely about incidents like this. I should
not myself have thought of the affair as an 'incident' at
all. It was a great bore.

I could see that Robinson was making an effort to form

some communal life for the period of our waiting on the island. I could see he conceived this a duty, and found it a nuisance. It had been different in the first few weeks, when we were impaired by the crash. Then Robinson had met the occasion. So, too, had Jimmie, who was now suffering belatedly; he kept insisting he had lost his nerves.

Robinson rose at five, we at six, by which time our plateau was flooded with the early sun, and not far below was the white mist, swathing the mountain right down to the coast. It seemed that the whole sky was beneath us and we on a sunny platform in space, with our house, mustard field, blue and green lake, the goat meadow before us and the mountain rising behind.

At this hour Robinson would go to the goat in its pen with a quantity of three-leaved plants, like large, leaved clover. These he had sprinkled with a considerable handful of salt.

'Why do you salt its food, Robinson?'

'It works up a thirst, and so increases the milk. Besides, it gives the milk a good salt flavour.'

It was one of the few bits of husbandry I saw Robinson practise. For the most part he made shift as easily as possible with tins and the derelict orchards of the croft.

I cooked the breakfast. Having found a sack of good oats in the storehouse I now made porridge every morning. Previously he and Miguel had eaten a mango or half paw-paw from one of the old croft orchards with a tin of baked beans. My institution of the porridge was designed to eke out the beans, for I saw that the stores were not large.

'Oh, when we've finished the beans we would go on to something else,' said Robinson; 'there are other tinned things.'

It was not only a matter of what was and was not proper for breakfast:

'Are you *sure* the pomegranate boat will come in August?'

44

'Quite sure.'

I did not care for the thought of its omitting to come and leaving the five of us tinless and starving. I did think Robinson might have grown something. The climate was suitable for maize, which is not troublesome. Fresh vegetables would have been no trouble. I decided to search the island for roots or berry-bushes which could be transplanted into Robinson's plateau. I was moody whenever I thought of the kitchen garden that Robinson did not have.

It is true that, with Robinson's makeshift system, the place was easy to run. As Tom Wells regained his health, our chores were finished by eleven in the morning. We took turns to prepare meals. The rest of the day we were free. We frequently quarrelled.

To my surprise, when we were sufficiently recovered and organized, and first sat down to meals together, Robinson said a prayer for grace. Despite the crucifixes on the walls of each room, I had not thought Robinson was a religious man; and I had vaguely supposed that the crucifixes had belonged to the previous owner, Robinson not troubling to remove them. I was even more surprised to observe that the form of grace he said was that used by Roman Catholics, 'Bless us, O Lord, and these Thy gifts. . . . In the name of the Father, the Son. . . .' And when we had finished he gave thanks according to the form used by English Catholics, following it with that usual prayer for the faithful departed which frequently suggests to my mind that we have eaten them.

I had entered the Catholic Church the previous year, I wondered if Robinson really was a member of the Church. But I do not care to ask people this question. I assumed, meantime, that he was so, and I wondered really why he chose to live so separated from the Sacraments; but that was his business.

After supper Robinson had us all into his sitting-room.

This was a strain. It never seemed to be the simple and normal thing for us to do. And I felt he did not so much invite as have us in, as one's headmistress would have one in to tea; an obligation on both sides.

Robinson encouraged a certain formality among us. We were as yet ignorant of each other's antecedents. Robinson did not ask any questions or lead us to talk about the circumstances which had brought us on the Lisbon plane, our homes, and destinations. I gathered from this that he was anxious to regard our intrusion into his life as temporary: once you know some facts about a person you are in some way involved with them. Evidently Robinson wished to avoid this. So did I. At first this reserve gave an illusion of natural growth to our relationships.

But of course the decent gulfs did not last. Sometimes it seemed that Robinson did not so much desire to preserve distance between us as to prevent intimacy; he seemed more anxious that we should not be friends than that we should not intrude upon each other. And, for many reasons, I did not want Robinson to know what Jimmie had told me about him.

In other ways, as I saw my companions day by day, I did begin to feel curiosity about them.

Sometimes in those evenings we would play chess. Robinson and I were more interested in chess than were Jimmie and Tom Wells who approached it as if it were some therapeutic task set by Robinson. They would talk too much.

'Look here,' Wells said one evening, 'where does this get us, anyway?'

'Is question you ask,' said Jimmie.

Robinson said pleasantly, 'Chess is good for the mind.'

'Look here,' Wells said, 'who are *you* to say what's good for *my* mind?'

I thought this reasonable enough. But I simply did not like Tom Wells. So I said, 'Oh, don't be difficult,' without looking up from the board where Robinson's King's Bishop, his only remaining protection, would threaten my Queen, should I move my King's Knight as I desired.

'Would you like to hear some music?' Robinson said.

He put a record on his gramophone. It was the first of six, a whole opera of Rossini, *La Cenerentola*.

I felt that Robinson was determined to keep control. He was fixed on controlling himself, us, and his island. He was not prepared to permit any bickering to bind us together and shatter the detachment which he prized.

Jimmie started to relax and listen politely. I did the same, though I felt a difficult mood begin to overtake me. I don't think Tom Wells had any intention of rudeness, it was only that he had never thought of music as anything but a background to talk. And more, not even a background; according to his notion, you had some music to take away the silence and then you continued talking, but in a louder voice.

'Ah, now,' said Wells, looking genially round the company, 'naturally this is a strain on us all, but we're lucky to be alive.'

He often said 'We're lucky to be alive' for no apparent reason save that he was pining to chew over and over our advent on the island, and thus for us all to get to grips with each other. 'It's unnatural living like this alone with Nature,' he would say, 'but we're lucky to be alive.' And sometimes he would bring out this phrase after he had spent half an hour calculating how much he was out of pocket through the plane mishap.

Perhaps there was nothing really objectionable about his 'lucky to be alive'. You must understand that I did not like Tom Wells.

'Amazing lucky shave,' said Wells. 'It's a remarkable thing, only that morning when I got my plane ticket at the Bureau I said –'

'Do you like Rossini?' said Robinson. He handed us glasses of rum for which I was most grateful at that moment.

'I hope this won't make me remiss,' said Tom Wells, holding his glass up to the lamp for some reason, and squinting at it with one eye. He said to me, 'Do you like cabaret?'

Robinson smiled weakly and sighed. At the sound of his sigh I suddenly decided to annoy him too.

'I love cabaret,' I said, 'if it's good.'

'A jolly good floor show,' said Tom Wells.

'Extremely nice,' I said. 'Do you know the Caribee Club in Duke Street?'

'Naturally,' said Wells.

'And the Daub and Wattle? They do a nice floor show there.'

'My word,' said Wells, 'we've got a lot in common, you and I.'

Robinson sat with his music, affronted. Serve you right, I thought, for your inflexible pose. Give you something, I thought, to exercise detachment upon.

'If I had the right music and a decent dress,' I said, 'I could perform a floor show all on my own.' It is true that I can do a rather effective song-and-dance turn, and often do, to amuse my intimate friends.

'Got any jazz?' Tom Wells said to Robinson, who was putting Rossini on the other side of the record.

He didn't answer.

Jimmie raised his eyebrows, and looked wise.

'You and I must have a chat,' said Wells to me.

Miguel was reclining on the hearth. He looked to one and the other of us, not following our actual conversation, but feeling out for himself how things stood between us all.

Jimmie sat like three wise monkeys, taking an occasional sip from his glass. It struck me he was secretly happy that Robinson was being slightly challenged and things were pepping up.

48

Presently Jimmie winked at Robinson who made no response, sitting vigilant by his gramophone, winding the handle every now and again, and replacing the records of his Rossini.

I left them, and went for a walk. My moods are not stable at the best of times. It was on this occasion I experienced that desire to worship the moon, and I thought, how remarkable, since I was a Christian: I thought of my grandmother bowing in the roadway, 'New Moon, New Moon, be good to me.'

After that, of course, I had difficulty in shaking off Tom Wells. He followed me about, as far as he was physically able. This was not very far; he was still fairly weak and still bound in his tight corset of canvas strips. He resented a great deal his injuries being more severe than Jimmie's or mine.

'You two were lucky,' he would say. 'That Robinson,' he would say, 'has no feelings or he wouldn't expect me to move about in my condition. It's not natural; I ought to be taking things easy.'

'You need exercise to avoid complications, Robinson says.'

'*Robinson says! Robinson says!* – Haven't you any guts?'

'It's his island.'

Robinson said to me 'He seems to want jazz music. I haven't any jazz.'

'He thinks you very unnatural,' I said, 'not having a wireless.'

'I can't please everybody,' Robinson said.

'I wish he would stop following me.'

'Your own fault,' said Robinson. 'You have to keep a man like that at a distance.'

'He has his funny side,' I said. 'Have you seen the stuff he keeps in that brief-case?'

It was in the heat of the day. I was peaceably watching

49

Robinson cleaning a gun. He stood in the cool stone room with his back to a vaulted window which blazed with light. When I mentioned Tom Wells he stopped cleaning the gun. He said, 'I've told him that we are none of us interested in the contents of his bag.'

'I am,' I said, 'very interested.'

'Not while you're on this island, you aren't,' said Robinson.

I had been sitting by a high table lolling with my elbows on it, but I stood up quickly. Robinson flung his rag on to the table and hanging up the gun on the wall, took down another.

'Try to conceal your anger,' said Robinson.

'I take an interest in what I please,' I said.

'Not while you're on this island.'

I left him, and went out to find Jimmie. On the way I took two cigarettes from the box on Robinson's desk. Thinking it over, I made some allowances for Robinson's behaviour, for he had recently been harassed by Wells. Only the previous day I had witnessed a scene between them, when Tom Wells had made a dreadful fuss about some documents which he said were missing from his brief-case.

'I say, Robinson, was this case open when you found it?'

'No, it was tight shut.'

'It must have been open,' said Wells. 'Some papers must have fallen out. Some important confidential documents. They're missing.'

'The bag was not open,' Robinson said steadily. 'It was lying about thirty yards from the plane near the spot where I picked you up.'

'The papers were in the case before the plane crashed. Now they're gone. How d'you explain that?'

'I am not an occulist,' Robinson said.

I found Jimmie on the patio reclining in a deck-chair beside

Tom Wells. Miguel was hovering near Tom Wells's chair, and I could not at first see what they were doing.

As I approached Wells looked round.

'Robinson there?' he said.

'No, he's cleaning the guns.'

'Makes no odds, really,' said Tom Wells. 'Only Robinson doesn't seem to care for these articles. He's a cranky bird if you like.'

I lit one of Robinson's cigarettes and felt in a position to defend him.

'That's a nice thing,' I said pompously, 'to say about your benefactor.'

'Look, Janey,' he said, 'all right, so what, let's put it at the maximum. O.K., Robinson saved my life. Does that give him the right to boss me around for three months?'

'It's Robinson's island,' I said.

Miguel gazed at us both, back and forth. Meantime I noticed, spread out on the flat of Tom Wells's bag, a number of small shining objects of curious shapes.

'I commence to think,' said Jimmie, 'that Robinson is becoming exceedingly cheesed.'

'*Pas devant*,' said Tom Wells, casting his eyes towards the child.

'Is not clandestine remark,' said Jimmie. 'I declare to Robinson's face the same.'

I began to scrutinize the curious objects of silver metal spread out on Tom Wells's bag. Miguel kept fingering them with delight.

'See,' said the boy to me, 'Mr Tom has given me one of his jewels.' It was a four-leaved clover, done in metal, attached to a chain. Miguel slung it round his neck.

'That will bring you luck,' said Tom Wells.

'What is luck?' said the boy, for although his pronunciation of English was good, his vocabulary was limited to what he had learned from Robinson.

Jimmie laughed. 'Is very humorous,' he said, 'that the youngster should ask what is luck. Robinson does not speak that word, he does not accord with the idea luck.'

'You seem to know a lot about Robinson,' Tom Wells observed.

'Is so,' said Jimmie genially. He had not confided to Tom Wells anything of a past association with Robinson, but I could see Wells suspected this. I imagined, and rightly, that Robinson had advised Jimmie not to talk much about himself.

'You would think to hear you,' said Wells, 'that Robinson was an old friend of yours, and you'd just dropped in.'

Tom Wells was more transparent than I was in his curiosity to know the story of Robinson's life. In time, I felt, bit by bit, the story would simply come to me. Jimmie would talk, Robinson would let fall; and so I asked few questions.

Tom Wells was constantly pestering us with questions. For my part, I was as close as Robinson. In fact, one of the few grounds on which I understood Robinson was the fear of over-familiarity which I shared with him. The less I said about my past life, the better, to Tom Wells, and on an island.

'It will bring me luck. What's luck?' Miguel was saying. He took the metal clover in his brown hands, raised it to his wide lips, and kissed it. 'What's luck?'

Jimmie and I were searching the air for a definition when 'Long life and happiness,' said Tom Wells.

'Now come over here, sonny, and I'll show you the signs of the Zodiac. When were you born?'

Miguel looked blank.

'What month?' said Tom. 'You don't have to give date and year. I shan't give you a comprehensive horoscope reading unless you're prepared to pay money for it, see? Got any money on you?'

I suppose he had a way with children.

Miguel fondled his clover charm, and giggled with delight.

'What month were you born?'

'Don't know.'

'When's your birthday, you daftie?'

'Next year.'

'What month? January, February, March, April ...? Come along – you pay your money and you take your choice.'

'January,' said Miguel, as if he were choosing a colour.

'Before or after the twenty-first?'

'Eh?'

'What date in January? First, second, third, fourth ...? Make up your mind.'

'First,' said Miguel.

'That's my birthday,' I said.

'No it is not,' said Miguel, 'it's mine.'

Jimmie said, 'Is humorous.'

'Look here,' said Wells to me, 'you can't have his birthday. His birthday's the first of January, see?'

Miguel danced round Wells, and picked up the glittering trinkets, one by one. Wells regarded him with the greatest benevolence. At that moment I realized that Tom Wells bore a strong resemblance to my brother-in-law, the bookie, Curly Lonsdale. He was about the same age as Curly, about fifty. Like Curly, Tom Wells had a loose mouth in a square puffy face, and would gesture continually with his square hands, fingers outspread. The over-intimate gurgle in the voice was the same as Curly's.

The first I had heard of Curly was when my sister Agnes wrote to me 'Julia has married such a common little man. He's a Turf Accountant. He looks like one of those that seduce landladies' daughters in their braces. Julia is of course lucky to marry anyone. . . .'

Years later, after my grandmother's funeral, I met Curly.

53

I was not surprised to find him fairly frightful, but I was enormously surprised, on this occasion and subsequently, to see how my son took to him. Brian delighted to go spinning off with Curly in his three-year-old Jaguar to the pictures on a Saturday afternoon. The first time, Brian was brought back at half-past eight, brimming with the exotic new world which he had tasted. 'Curly was carrying seven hundred and fifty on him, he showed me, great bundles of fivers . . . and after the pictures we had fish and chips in a pretty nice restaurant at Leicester Square, and after that we went to a house to meet a lot of Curly's friends. They were all playing cards, and there were piles and piles of cigarette ends in the ashtrays and fivers all over the place. And the chaps were terribly keen on the game, they had their coats off –'

'Sitting in their braces,' I said.

'That's right. And Curly's going to take me to the races when the season starts.'

'Did they give you anything to drink?' I said.

'Oh yes. There was ginger ale. Sam – that's one of Curly's friends – gave Curly a snifter – that's brandy, you see, and I think he was pouring out one for me, but Curly said, "Something soft for the youngster, Sam, else his old woman's going to create." That was awfully funny, because Curly winked at me; and he looked awfully funny.'

'Were there any ladies?'

'No,' said Brian. 'No dames. But there was a photo of a smasher on the grand piano.'

'Do you really like Curly?' I said.

'He's the best man in our family,' said Brian, as if there were dozens to choose from. Apart from Curly Lonsdale the only other man in our family was Agnes's husband, the doctor, Ian Brodie. From any point of view, it seemed to me, Curly was preferable to Ian. One of the things that worried me, as I sat on the patio watching Tom Wells, so like my brother-in-law Curly, winning his way with Miguel,

54

was who had taken charge of Brian since I had been presumed dead; Agnes and Ian Brodie, or Julia and Curly? On the whole, I hoped it was Curly, whom I could never, myself, take to.

'This is Ethel of the Well,' said Tom Wells, picking out one of his trinkets. It was a large-headed female figure. Its mouth was cut wide from ear to ear, its arms stuck flat against its metal sides, and from under the lines of its long straight skirt protruded the representation of a pair of thick curling boots. 'The original Ethel,' said Wells, 'was found in a well in Somerset. She dates back to the sixth century. Ethel has terrific properties as a luck bringer; I could show you hundreds of letters from people whose life has been changed by Ethel.'

Miguel let the four-leaved clover drop on his breast and made a dive at Ethel of the Well. 'When I think,' said Tom Wells, 'of the business I'm losing. There's the magazine also, who's taken it over? I've got the proofs of the June number here. Well, we're lucky to be alive.' He fumbled in his bag. 'Listen to this letter from a satisfied customer: "Dear Mr Wells, My wife and I would like to tell you that we have had incredible luck since you sent us Ethel of the Well. Ethel is certainly the tops. My wife was dogged by ill health for twelve years. Now I have got a better job, and we certainly swear by Ethel. Wishing you congrats and all the best from my wife and I, Yours faithfully, Mr & Mrs Harper." That's only one out of hundreds from simple ordinary folk. I get a lot of confidences, too. People must open their hearts to someone, mustn't they? I know thousands of secrets – some of them would open your eyes. Rich and poor alike, they write to Tom Wells.'

'Ethel!' said Miguel in hushed awe.

'Then there's Natty the Gnome,' said Wells.

'Show me Natty,' said Miguel.

'To Natty,' said Wells, 'I owe the fact that I am here to

55

tell the tale. Mind you, it isn't the first time Natty has saved a life in an accident. I wish I had the letter here –'

'It would have been luckier if there had been no accident,' I said.

'There must have been a Jonah on the plane. You are powerless when there's a Jonah.'

'Show me Natty,' said Miguel.

Wells selected from his wares a small charm and handed it to the child. 'You can keep that,' he said, 'I've got others.' It was a dwarf-like figure with a peaked cap sitting cross-legged. 'Thank God for Natty,' he said. 'I've always had faith in Natty. We must be losing thousands of orders.'

I could see Jimmie was as envious as I was of Tom Wells's salvage. All our possessions had been burnt up in the plane, and we had no form of competition for the attention of Miguel.

'There was to be a full-page ad for Natty in the June number of *Your Future*,' said Wells.

'Show me the Future,' said Miguel.

'Letters pour in daily from every part of the world from thousands of men and women of all ages,' Wells said, 'in praise of Natty the Gnome and affiliated products.'

'Mayhaps they now shall cease to write,' said Jimmie, 'when they hear of your bad luck which has befallen.'

'What bad luck?' said Wells aggressively.

'Show me the Future,' said Miguel, apparently under the impression it was one of the metal charms.

'Let him see the magazine,' I said.

Wells carefully placed his range of lucky charms on the patio floor; he fished emotionally into his bag and produced a paste-up proof of his magazine, which he held sorrowfully before his eyes.

'What's going to happen about *Your Future* I don't know,' he said. 'The June number won't appear, naturally, because this here in my hand is the June number. I prepared it while on tour, and I intended to mail it from Santa Maria to our offices in Paddington. What they are doing at Paddington, I don't know, I dare not think.'

'Mayhaps they all pack up,' said Jimmie.

'They won't,' said Wells, 'not while I'm alive they won't.'

'By now you must be presumed dead,' I said, 'like the rest of us.'

'*They* will know,' said Wells. 'Trust them. They know I'm alive, you can be sure.'

'They know all about Mr Tom,' said Miguel, who seemed to feel that his friend was under attack.

'You see,' said Tom, 'I have friends among the Occult. There's no getting away from it; they know what's going on in the world. I'm not talking about a lot of ignorant fortune-tellers, mind you; these are scientists of every description and in every sense of the word. Some of them have letters after their names. They are people that have devoted their lives to the study of the unknown. I am not an adherent, mind you, of any particular group. There are countless methods of probing the mysteries of the universe. I number among my acquaintances distinguished psychometrists, clairvoyants, Karma interpreters, astrologers, yoga spiritualists, divine healers, astral radiesthetists, saliva prognosticators, and so on and so on. They are men and women of vision. It's the quality of the medium that counts, naturally. I go in for quality. All my friends are of high esoteric quality.'

He lapsed into a sigh of exhaustion, content merely to spread his square hands palm-up before him, as if they spoke for his cause.

'Mr Tom's friends know,' said Miguel.

'Listen to the innocent child,' said Tom Wells. 'He's got the right ideas, that boy.'

'Is this the Future?' said Miguel, holding up a medallion with cabbalistic signs in red enamel round its perimeter.

'That's the Chaldean Contact Medallion, sonny. You've picked a winner there. Real enamel lettering. Astounding potency, and puts an end to ill health, exhaustion, fatigue, insomnia, etcetera. It is also an infallible aid to joyous achievement. You can also keep that one, I've got plenty.'

'Show him the magazine,' I said, 'that's what he's asking for.'

Tom Wells frowned surreptitiously at me. 'It's a bit beyond him,' he whispered. '*Your Future* is mainly for those who have passed through the early talismanic stages of spiritual attainment.' He tapped his sheaf of papers. 'We have serious articles here,' he said, 'by professors.'

'Give me *Your Future*,' said Miguel.

'Give him *Your Future*,' I said.

'It's only in proof form,' said Wells. 'He won't understand it. It's my only copy. He has the charms, that's sufficient.'

Miguel seemed to feel a sense of deprivation.

'I want *Your Future*,' he observed to me.

'For shame,' said Jimmie, 'withholding these documents from the little child.'

'He can have it to look at,' said Wells, 'but I want it back, mind, and I don't mean maybe.'

Miguel grabbed the pasted-up proofs and started turning the pages. He seemed to be attracted by the pictures in the advertisements, but did not waste time on the text.

'I told you,' said Wells, 'it wouldn't interest the child.'

Miguel sensed that his treasure was about to be removed. He clutched it to his chest and said, 'It's mine.'

'No,' said Wells, 'give it back.'

'Is cruelty,' said Jimmie, 'to give to a child and then withdraw.'

At that moment Robinson appeared. Miguel hastily grabbed from the step where he had laid them his three lucky charms, and clutched them fiercely, together with *Your Future*.

'What the hell's going on here?' said Robinson. He was looking at the litter of lucky charms on the floor of the patio around Tom Wells where he had laid them out.

Tom Wells placed a hand on his ribs to indicate pain.

'This is Mr Wells's range of samples,' I said. 'They are all vibrating with luck.'

'I was decent enough to hand over that rubbish to you,' Robinson said to Wells, 'on condition you kept it to yourself.'

Tom Wells closed his eyes and rubbed his ribs.

I picked up one of the charms. 'This one is Ethel of the Well,' I said, 'guaranteed to –'

'What have you got there?' Robinson was looking at Miguel.

The boy handed over the proofs, keeping the charms clenched in his other hand.

Robinson tore the proofs several times across. We all gasped.

Eventually Wells said, 'That's an actionable offence. If there wasn't a lady present I'd tell you what I think of you. That's my property you've destroyed. And while we're on the subject I'd like to know what's happened to the papers that are missing from my case. They were top secret.'

Robinson said to Miguel, 'What have you got there?'

The child opened his hand and showed him the charms.

'Give them back to Mr Tom,' said Robinson, quite nicely.

'They're mine,' said Miguel.

'They are harmless things,' I said.

'They bring you luck,' said the boy.

'Listen to me, Miguel: these are evil things,' said Robinson, 'you must give them back.'

Miguel said, 'It's cruelty to give to a child and then withdraw.'

'Is humorous,' said Jimmie.

Robinson looked round at us and said, 'You are clearly in the wrong, as my guests, to alienate the child.'

'Give those articles to Mr Tom like a most noble youth,' said Jimmie to Miguel.

The child began to cry at this first sign of desertion.

'Give them back to me for the meantime,' said Wells. 'I'll keep them for you.'

'You must not subject the boy to trickery,' said Robinson. 'He must know I don't permit him to have them at all.'

Wells tried again, 'Give the lucky charms to Robinson,' he said, 'and they may bring him some luck.'

Miguel cheered up. 'Robinson can have one of them,' he said. 'Robinson can have the medal for luck, I'll keep Ethel and Natty and I don't mean maybe.'

'I shall not keep it for luck,' said Robinson ruthlessly. 'I shall throw it into the Furnace over the mountain. You see, Miguel, these bits of metal are full of harm.' As he looked at them lying in the boy's palm, I caught an expression of nausea on Robinson's face. I thought to myself, 'He really believes they have evil properties.'

'Miguel,' I said, 'give them all back to Mr Tom, and presently we shall give you something better to make up.' I wondered desperately what we could give him.

'You must not mislead,' said Robinson. 'The fact is, you have nothing to give him. Apart from this rubbish of Wells's, and the clothes you wear, you are all, for the time being, destitute.'

The boy was mildly weeping again. I said, 'You ought not to torment him with all this argument.'

'Well,' said Robinson, 'I shall not take the things from him by force. In any case, I wouldn't care to handle them.'

'That's rather superstitious of you,' I said.

I could see that Robinson was furious. As if retorting to a challenge, he lifted up a few of the charms from the patio and examined them. He really hated handling them.

Suddenly he poured them into Wells's lap and said, 'Bella is sick, Miguel. Come and have a look at her.' Bella was the goat. 'Bella,' said Miguel. He followed Robinson, putting the amulets in his pocket.

'There's something wrong with that man,' said Tom Wells.

'It's Robinson's island,' I said.

'I'm a British citizen,' said Wells. 'He has destroyed my property. Those are the simple facts; I'll take it up with the authorities when we get home.'

He started picking up the pieces of his magazine. This was difficult owing to his encased ribs. Jimmie and I scrambled round trying to help him. When we had gathered all the bits I had an idea, and obtained some transparent sticky tape from Robinson's desk.

I brought this out to the patio and set about piecing the torn pages together like a jigsaw. Like Miguel, I found the advertisement section with its supporting photographs the most alluring. There was an intense turbanned Indian, a scholarly fellow in horn-rimmed glasses, a motherly soul, a good-looking young man in a monk's cowl, a wild-eyed girl resembling Emily Brontë, all accompanied by appropriate announcements, which also fascinated me.

BARI SAWIMI can provide Tactile Regeneration. Send fragment of Personal Garb, cloth 3″ x 7″ for immediate postal reply & satisfaction. P.O. 37s. 6d. no cheques to 'Bari Sawimi', Box 957 *Your Future*.

MURIEL THE MARVEL with her X-ray eyes. *Can read your very soul*. Scores of satisfied clients. . . .

CONSULT BROTHER DEREK. Troubled? Anxious? Is that well-paid job just out of your reach? Write to Brother Derek. . . .

I discovered in one of the pictures a touched-up likeness of Wells himself, entitled Dr Benignus.

Trust Dr Benignus. Treat him as your Father. Free advice to all readers of *Your Future* and members of the Dr Benignus Magic Circle of Friendship. Financial, Matrimonial, and Moral Problems treated in Strictest Confidence. Dr Benignus has brought Consolation and Happiness to Thousands. . . .

At last I had the proofs complete, though ragged.

'That's sweet of you, honey,' said Wells.

'Is not to call Miss January honey,' said Jimmie, 'as if she was a trumpet, and any –'

'You mean strumpet,' I said.

'Strumpet,' said Jimmie, 'and any indignities vented upon this lady, I black your eye full sore.'

Tom Wells clasped his ribs, closed his eyes, and addressed me: 'To be serious for a moment, there's an article in this issue that will appeal to you. See page twelve. It's called "Are We Fulfilling the Prediction of the Apocalypse?"'

'Is serious,' said Jimmie.

'Naturally,' said Wells, 'it's extremely serious.'

'I mean, that I black your eye,' said Jimmie.

Chapter 6

To reach the other side of the island there was no way but over the mountain. From our plateau it rose steeply, but the path wound to east and north-east, cutting off the higher reaches, and descending through stretches of squelchy moss on the lava rocks, through juniper woods to a green plain at the North Arm. At some points on the path where the clumps of juniper lay above, and only a thin white sunlight penetrated the clouds, the scene was sharp, its dark and light the texture of a woodcut. In direct sunlight a variety of greens twinkled suddenly, glimpses of mossy craters. Curious red lights appeared, which I later discovered were caused by vapours rising from the soil like rusty dew. To the west of this route the mountain was pitted with deep wide craters. The shallower pits were filled with iridescent blue and green pools. This was the moonish landscape of which Robinson had spoken. The feel of the earth underfoot, the colours, even the air, were strange.

I have never seen so many mountain springs. Robinson said these little brooks were constantly appearing, so that every time he crossed the mountain, which was about every month, he would notice some two or three new springs. At a point just above our plateau, where the rock was uncovered and the sun particularly strong, I saw a small cactus type of plant, and, from the wedge of rock where the cactus had taken root, and as if from the plant itself, a small stream bubbling with force. This was on the occasion of my first crossing the mountain. I was with Robinson, who was bound for a certain mineral spring which contained strong healing properties; he thought it might cure his

63

sick goat. Robinson was very taken by the sight of the water apparently gushing from the cactus. 'That's a new spring,' he said. He left me there and went back to the house to get his camera. I still have the print of the photograph. It looks a fake, the cactus opening its thick lips, like a carved fountain gryphon, to disgorge a stream of water.

Robinson walked ahead. He addressed me over his shoulder,

'Are you keeping up your journal?'

'No, I've lost interest lately.'

'You should write it up every day.'

'I don't care for it. I may continue later.'

'You should care for it. I thought you were a writer.'

'You don't catch me writing anything unless it suits me,' I said.

'Ah,' he said, 'I see. You write for pleasure. Taken to its logical conclusion your attitude –'

'Look at the mimosa clump,' I said. There was a coppice on a plateau below us, and at its edge about six mimosa trees. I am always angered when people say to me, 'Taken to its logical conclusion your attitude . . .'

'Keep up your journal,' he said. 'It will take your mind off Jimmie.'

'I don't see that I want to keep my mind off Jimmie,' I said.

Of course, working over this conversation later, in my fury, I regretted not having replied, 'You are insolent', or something like that.

Jimmie and I had been planning an expedition over the mountain, and after some hesitation we had consulted Robinson about the route. I had, in fact, attempted to pump Miguel as to the best way across the mountain, but 'Ask Robinson,' he said.

'I don't suppose there's anything worth seeing on the mountain,' I said purposely.

Miguel laughed, and then to give me something to think about he said,

'There are three secret tunnels.'

'I'll believe them when I see them,' I said.

'Ask Robinson,' he said.

Jimmie and I did not particularly want to ask Robinson. We would have preferred to set out on our own, for we felt that Robinson would somehow contrive not to take us both together. As it transpired, this was true. Robinson had made it clear that he was not in favour of my friendship with Jimmie. Now it is true that I was becoming rather attached to Jimmie, mostly because of our situation on the island, and the qualities of the island, the colours and the atmospherics and mists, and that sort of thing.

One afternoon when Tom Wells was sleeping, Robinson and Miguel fishing in one of the streams above our plateau, I said to Jimmie, 'Let's get out of this.'

'Whither?' said Jimmie.

'Over the mountain, perhaps?'

He shook his head. 'I know not the mountain.'

'What other parts of the island do you know?' I said.

'The burial ground,' he said.

Robinson had promised to show us all of the island. It was now our eighth week. My only excursion had been that to the beach by the southern path. Tom Wells, partly because of his injury and partly because of a lazy incuriosity, did not attempt to explore very much; I thought he seemed to wish to reproduce about himself as far as possible the environment of his magazine office at Paddington. Robinson had put a desk in his room, where he had his papers spread before him and wrote articles for forthcoming numbers of *Your Future* on paper sadly provided by Robinson. Sometimes he read such of Robinson's books as would hold his attention. He complained much of the food, the climate, and the money he was losing by his incarceration on the island – that is how he expressed it. 'This enforced incarceration,' he said every day, along with other often repeated phrases such as 'My wife's gone over to her sister's, I dare say', 'We're lucky to be alive', and 'There's something unnatural about that Robinson'. He complained, too, of Robinson's having wheedled the trinkets out of Miguel and cast them in a live crater known as the Furnace: 'That Robinson's a religious maniac', or 'That man goes crazy if you give the child a kind look'.

On one occasion when Robinson had been particularly irritated by my winning Miguel's praise for a very fine ping-pong match with Bluebell, it occurred to me that I, compared with Robinson, Jimmie, and Tom Wells, was bearing up pretty well in the circumstances. Having mused thus, I immediately helped myself to four of Robinson's share of the cigarettes, to safeguard my soul against the deadly sin of pride. It is really mortifying to do a small mean injury to someone; but a theologian once told me that this is not sound doctrine.

Jimmie observed my theft, and while I lit up and luxuriously puffed one of the plundered cigarettes I explained the motive to Jimmie. It was then, it being the early afternoon and Tom Wells being asleep, that I said, 'Let's get out of this.' We planned an excursion for the following day. Jimmie led the way to the burial ground which lay slightly to the north-west of our plateau, less than a mile from the house. We had a short steep climb; after that the downward slope was easy. On the western side of the mountain there were a few lava pits, but not nearly so many as I subsequently saw on my north-eastern crossing with Robinson. I was surprised to see that the plane had been wrecked, not on one of the hefty cliff faces of our mountain, but on a gentle green hillside, merging into downland. Here, on the night of the crash, Robinson had found us, Jimmie wandering in a daze with blood running down his face, I unconscious and lying still as death on my side, Tom Wells groaning and twisting by the light of the blazing plane. Eventually, as dawn broke, and Jimmie was calmed, he and Robinson had carried us to the shore of the green and blue lake.

Quite nearby, in a flat-bottomed hollow, Jimmie and Robinson had buried the dead, and lest the graves were not deep enough – since two grave-diggers for the remains of twenty-six dead are too few for deep digging – they had unsettled a number of rock boulders and lava lumps from the sides of the mound surrounding the hollow, rolling them down into the graveyard. These newly uprooted rocks, some a sort of porous red and some black lava, littered the hollow, protecting the burial ground from disturbances of mist and rain, until the pomegranate men should arrive in August and perhaps be persuaded to work over the graves, thus to give the bodies more security.

Sometimes, on the plateau where Robinson's house stood, when the wind was from the north or east, a curious smell of burning would pervade the atmosphere, penetrating the rooms. It was sulphurous. Robinson said it came from a bubbling eruption still lively on the mountain, which he called the Furnace.

'I should like to see the Furnace,' I said.

'I will take you there, one day.'

Whenever the wind was north-east, bringing the burning sulphur smell, I had reminded him of his promise.

Sitting with Jimmie above the burial ground I noticed a burnt-out smell, although there was no wind.

'There must be a molten lava pit nearby,' I said.

'Is the odours of the aeroplane which you smell,' said Jimmie. He rose and beckoned to me. I followed him down the hill and there, to our left, lay the wreck of the plane, reclining on its grassy slope, and still, after eight weeks, giving off a smell of burning as a dead fire-eating dragon might smell in its decay.

When I saw the wreck I started to cry. Jimmie said, 'Ah me! Partake of a drop of brandy.' Even so, I could not stop crying, even though I giggled at Jimmie's words, and even though I had already, many times since my recovery from the accident, pictured to my mind the scene of the wreck, attempting to realize it as an exercise for pity, since pity is an emotion which does not come easily in the bewilderment and first fears of a very strange environment.

I do not know whether it was for pity that I wept at the sight of the wreck, only that I could not stop crying. We walked on until both the wreck and the burial ground were concealed behind a grassy hump, and we settled, watching the sea shimmering below us, but still I went on crying.

We had a picnic pack with us – two guavas, some banana cream biscuits, and a bottle filled with the pale yellow mineral water which Robinson and Miguel frequently brought from the mountain. Jimmie opened the pack and poured out a drink for me into an enamel mug. Although I was crying hard I thought it looked yellower than usual, and when I tasted it, I said, 'What have you put in it?' recognizing the taste and glow of brandy.

'Where did you get the brandy?' I said, at the same time weeping away.

Jimmie took his leather and silver flask from his jacket pocket and held it to my nose. 'I give you a drop more should you desire.'

'Where did you get it?'

'Is personal gift which I have received from a kinsman. When I am salvaged from the aeroplane, so also is my worthy flask.'

I did remember Jimmie's flask in the plane, and his sharing his brandy with me there. I said, dabbing my eyes, 'Where did you get the brandy – I know that the flask is yours, but where did you get the brandy?' For, on the plane, Jimmie and I had emptied his flask between us.

Jimmie looked lovingly at the flask, smelt it, and then, placing it next his ear, swilled it round to hear the splash of liquor.

'Is salvage,' he said. 'Alas, drink up and weep no more.'

I knew it was not salvage from the plane. The few battered bits of luggage that had been found in the vicinity of the wreck had been examined and labelled by Robinson, and some of the clothes distributed to Tom Wells and Jimmie for their present needs, I refusing such creepy garments. Certainly, there was no liquor intact in those far-flung battered and pathetic suitcases.

'Salvage from where?' I said, with my simply physical tears streaming. 'From Robinson?' I said.

And I said, 'Look here, Jimmie, this is Robinson's brandy. You shouldn't take Robinson's brandy.'

'Is in order to mortify my immortal soul, I help myself,' said Jimmie, 'like you have declared to me. And after all, bloody hell, a little of that which you fancy does good things to one.' He took a spotted silk scarf from his neck and gave it over to me to use for a handkerchief, since my own was wet with my crying. He poured himself out a portion of new brandy. I did not notice at the time, but realized later that the scarf was salvage. Meantime, I used it to cry into.

Jimmie lay back on his elbows and sipped.

'Many times past when Robinson has been old buddy of mine –' But he stopped, and presently he said,

'Robinson approaches.'

I looked up, and saw Robinson's head bobbing behind a hill some distance away, then, after a space, his head and shoulders behind a nearer mound, until gradually he wholly appeared, climbing up to our picnic place.

'What are you crying for?' he said, looking from me to Jimmie and then back at me.

I giggled, without stopping crying, at his suspicious look. I did quite like Robinson, but lately in his anxiety to keep order on his island he had seemed to me rather quaint.

'She laments for the aeroplane disaster, I guess,' said Jimmie leaning still on his elbows and sipping the brandy.

It did not sound quite convincing, which caused me to giggle again. At this Robinson looked hard at me, and then he said, 'Take some brandy.' And still looking closely at me he addressed Jimmie, 'Give her some brandy.' This surprised us both, for he had not seemed to have observed the flask cup in Jimmie's hand, far less that it contained brandy.

'I have some here,' I said, holding up the enamel mug.

Robinson put his nose inside.

'What's that mixture?'

'Mineral water and a dash of –'

'Not my *best* brandy?' said Robinson.

'Is so, naturally. Have sense,' said Jimmie.

'Do you mean to say,' said Robinson, 'that you have put my best brandy into mineral water? No wonder January is crying.'

I understood that he was making this fuss about his best brandy to save us the embarrassment of the question why we had his brandy at all, and I thought it rather nice of him.

'It tastes very good with mineral water,' I said.

The tears continued to pour from my eyes.

'Is woeful,' said Jimmie.

Robinson sat down beside us. He said to Jimmie:

'Any left in the flask?'

'Plenty.'

Jimmie handed him the flask. Robinson passed it to me and told me to take a good swig, which I did.

The brandy glow, almost like an emotion itself, began to spread within me. I felt it was demanded that I should say something about my crying. I did not know what to say. I thought of saying 'I feel such a fool,' but stopped myself, reflecting that women usually say this when they cry. I said, 'Oh dear, I don't know what to say.' But this sounded to me the depth of inanity.

'Try a cigarette,' said Robinson, and offered me his open cigarette case.

'No,' I said, '*you* have one of *mine*.' I fished into our picnic pack and brought out the envelope in which I kept my cigarettes.

'All right, I *will*,' said Robinson. '*Many* thanks.' Not that I cared much, I was too absorbed in my crying.

It stopped for a bit, while I smoked the cigarette.

'I wish I had some make-up for my face,' I said, trying to think up and utter some concrete complaint. And it was true that while I was on the island I greatly missed my make-up; I do not care to go about with nothing on my face so that everyone can see what is written on it. One of the day-dream fantasies that came to me like homesickness when I was on the island, was a make-up session. In my mind, I would be in my bedroom at home, performing the smoothing and creaming and painting of my face, going through the whole ritual of smoothing and patting, down to the last touch of mascara, taking my leisure, one hour, two hours. Whereas in reality, at home, I make up my face rather quickly, and only when, rarely, the idea seizes me, do I make a morning of it.

'We have some stuff among the salvage,' said Robinson. 'You could use that, if you feel it absolutely necessary.'

'No fear,' I said, and started to cry again.

'It isn't absolutely necessary,' said Robinson.

'Is essential,' said Jimmie, 'for a lady that she adorn her visage with a bit of paint.'

'Simply and factually it isn't essential,' said Robinson, 'but I have no objection to it.'

How it annoyed me when Robinson stated what he had or hadn't objections to! I stopped crying. I said, 'Your objections aren't in question.' I started to pack our bag as a sign that the picnic was over. It was not the first time that Robinson had intruded when Jimmie and I were out picnicking.

Robinson, as if he knew what was in my mind, said to Jimmie, 'I came to tell you about Bella. She's been vomiting. Milk her as usual but throw away the milk in case it is infected.'

He hurried on ahead while Jimmie and I followed. We stopped to watch the mist as it began to form, swirling like curdled milk below us.

It was the afternoon of the next day that I crossed the mountain with Robinson to procure mineral water for the goat. Jimmie had wanted to accompany us but Robinson had found an emergency to prevent him: dampness in the storehouse. All the packages had to be moved, and the piping behind one of the walls replaced.

'Keep up your journal; it will keep your mind off Jimmie.'

To which, of course, I should have replied, 'You are insolent.'

And while I answered, 'I don't see that I want to keep my mind off Jimmie', I was wondering how best, during the five weeks remaining to me on the island, to preserve some freedom from Robinson's interference in the matter of Jimmie, while retaining his protection from Wells.

Robinson inquired: 'Has Jimmie told you much about himself?'

I said, 'Jimmie has told me a lot about you.'

'What has Jimmie told you?' I expected that question. Looking round, I saw Miguel above and behind us, following. Watching him, I sorted out my few sensations, and

72

noted, one, that Miguel must have approached subterraneously, and, two, that I felt rather sorry for Robinson. It is hard for a recluse, and such an upright one, to feel his seclusion threatened by others' knowing a little about him.

'Here comes Miguel,' I said.

Robinson made an effort to look interested in Miguel's approach, then he casually repeated, 'What has Jimmie told you?' He gave an amused chuckle, as if to say, whatever he has told you isn't to be taken seriously.

'Hallo there, Miguel,' I shouted. The truth is, I have a sharp tongue when I am annoyed, and it is better to say anything beside the point rather than what I might say, at such moments, pointedly.

Miguel was grinning happily as he clambered behind us.

'You came by a secret tunnel,' I observed to him.

Robinson looked surprised for a second, then defeated, as if his last friend had betrayed him. It is always the same with people who make a fetish of self-control: they strike the most histrionic attitudes. How was I to know that the existence of the underground channels was supposed to be a secret?

Fortunately Miguel did not seem embarrassed by my remark.

'From this point,' said Robinson, who was a little way above me, 'you get a sight of the sea on both sides: Vasco da Gama's Bay on the north, and our Pomegranate Bay on the south. I call it the Pomegranate Bay because that's where the pomegranate boat puts in.'

It was, very much, a splendid sight. I was prepared to say no more on the troublesome subject of the underground caves, but Miguel devilishly put in, 'I know all the secret tunnels on the island.'

'I should like to see them,' I said.

'They are nothing much,' said Robinson, 'they are slimy holes in the mountain. In one of them there's a point where

73

you have to crawl on your stomach. And they are, of course, no longer secret.'

'She doesn't *know* them,' said Miguel.

'I only know of them,' I said.

'She doesn't know the secret tunnels,' said Miguel again with delight.

'I can smell the Furnace,' I said. I could also hear the rumbling, and presently I saw the red earthy smoke rising in puffs on the far side of a hill.

On the side of the crater from which we approached, the slope leading to its pit was fairly gradual, covered with tropical foliage, plants thick as ox tongues, but green from the numerous rivulets that scored this bank. As these streams of water reached the bottom of the crater they sizzled and steamed, this sound and vapour mixing with the rumble and sulphurous clouds of the eruption. The far wall of the crater was steep and sheer, and it was against this cliff that the breakers of red cloud beat and dispersed so that we could stand on the lip of the crater at our side watching the bubbling opposite, without much discomfort. From where we stood it would have been easy to walk down or slide into the bottom. But from the opposite edge it was a sheer drop.

'How awful to fall in,' I said. 'No one would survive it.'

Robinson said, 'The body would be sucked under immediately. There is a continuous action of suction and rejection going on down there.' He added, 'Curiously, if you throw in anything sizeable the eruption gives out a sort of scream. There must be a narrow tubular shaft leading down from the pit of the crater, and the suction action through this narrow pipe causes the sound, do you see?' I didn't see but I lifted the biggest stone I could manage, and sent it rolling into the milling mud. It gave out a very dreadful scream.

'Sometimes,' said Robinson, 'without provocation it sighs.'

'I should like to hear it sigh,' I said.

Miguel was half-way down the bank, picking some large-petalled flowers which seemed to have been by their original nature blue, but through the constant activity of red vapour had evolved to streaky mauve.

'Don't go too far, Miguel,' Robinson called. 'It's slippery farther down, and you might find yourself sliding in. We shan't come and drag you back.'

Miguel laughed. He said, 'The flowers are for Mr Tom.'

On the way back, Robinson once more referred to my journal.

'Keep it up. You will be glad of the notes later on. After all, you did intend to write about islands.'

'Not this island,' I said.

'Man proposes and God disposes,' he said.

I thought, there's something in that, and a pity you don't keep it in mind when your own scheme of things is upset.

I had been commissioned to write about islands in a series which included books about threes of everything. Three rivers, three lakes, and threes of mountains, courtesans, battles, poets, old country houses. I was supposed to be doing Three islands. Two of my chosen islands I already knew well: Zanzibar and Tiree. I had thought one of the Azores would complete an attractive trio. Someone else, now, has written the book on Three Islands. I believe someone has added to the series Three Men in My Life.

Robinson continued to harp on the advantages of my keeping a journal. My anger had dwindled to nothing at the sight of the Furnace, and in a more congenial humour I said, 'Oh well, I'll see.'

'Stick to facts,' said Robinson. 'There's the Furnace for one. And there are so many curious things on the island – the moths, have you noticed? And those very long lizards, the trees, those miniature junipers in the stunted part of the mountain, the ferns.'

I thought, 'And the derelict croft, the lack of cultivation.'

As if I had said it, he continued,

'You have not seen my pomegranate orchard.'

'No,' I said. 'Perhaps you'll take us there.'

He was silent for the rest of the journey home.

Chapter 7

BLUEBELL was chasing butterflies on the patio. Tom Wells was indoors sitting in his braces. Jimmie was with Robinson repairing the leaky pipe behind the storehouse. Miguel was sitting at the kitchen table doing his arithmetic. I sat in the sun, extremely tired in my bones after the crossing of the mountain on the previous day. I was making an entry in my journal:

Wednesday, 30th June – Robinson was born at Gibraltar in 1903, of a wealthy military family. He was educated in England and France. Then, about the age of twenty-four he entered an Irish seminary to study for the priesthood. This was highly regarded by his widowed mother, a Catholic, whose only child Robinson was. His father had been killed in 1917.

After a period in the seminary, and just before he was due to become a Deacon, Robinson refused to be ordained. He travelled in Spain, Italy, and South America, making observations of Catholic practices, and at the end of a year he left the Church on account of what he considered its superstitious character. In particular he objected to the advancing wave of devotion to the Blessed Virgin, and to this effect he wrote many letters to Catholic papers and articles later collected into a book entitled *The Dangers of Marian Doctrine*. Still professing the Catholic faith himself, Robinson maintained that the Church had fallen into heresy.

Robinson fought with the Republicans in Spain, but suffered a revulsion and deserted after six months. He then retired to Mexico, where he lived on a deserted ranch for some ten years.

In 1946 Robinson's mother died. He returned to bury her. He entrusted his considerable fortune to an uncle resident in Gibraltar with interests in Tangier. He bought this island which was then called Ferreira, from a Portuguese called Ferreira. He has been living here ever since.

His full name is Miles Mary Robinson. For some reason not clear to me one does not call him Mr Robinson, nor imagine anyone calling him Miles.

I sat limply in the cane chair, exhausted by this assembling of facts. I had enjoyed the small catty task – since by his 'stick to facts' Robinson had not meant facts about himself – and now obtained satisfaction from the thought, 'He has got what he asked for', but I could not rest in this simple thought. I was not even certain at this time whether all these facts were true. I had got them from Jimmie.

I was wondering again which of my sisters would consider herself Brian's guardian. He had recently gone away to school, and it was a question whether, when the summer holidays started, he would reside in the home of Curly Lonsdale or Ian Brodie.

I had seen, lying on Robinson's desk, his publication *The Dangers of Marian Doctrine*, with pages of pencilled addenda on which he was apparently still working.

My brother-in-law Ian, a Catholic from the time of his birth, and rather aggressive about his religion, was always using that word, danger, in connexion with Our Blessed Lady, though for my part I did not see the connexion. On returning from his continental holidays Ian frequently wrote to the Catholic newspapers letters of concern about the Marian excesses he had witnessed at feast-day processions in Italy or Spain, and their danger. What, he once demanded of me, were the bishops thinking of to permit these dangerous extravagances?

'I don't know, Ian,' I said, 'what bishops think of, for I don't know any bishops.'

'Any good Catholic,' said Ian, 'should be horrified to see the Mother of God worshipped as if she were a pagan goddess.'

'Do you believe in pagan goddesses?' I said. 'Do you believe they exist, have power?'

'Well, in the psychological sense –'

'I mean, in the real substantial sense.'

'No, not exactly.'

'Then I don't see the danger. Prayers addressed to the Blessed Virgin are not likely to be received by pagan goddesses.'

'There's a question of distortion of doctrine,' said Ian. 'These people make more fuss of the Blessed Virgin than of Jesus Christ. That's *dangerous*. And it's becoming prevalent all over the world. I've just written a letter –'

'I don't see that devotions to the Blessed Virgin are likely to be rewarded with the gift of corrupt doctrine.'

'It puts people off the Faith,' said Ian.

'What people?'

'Non-Catholics, lapsed Catholics, respectable Christians. . . .'

'There's always a stumbling-block. If it isn't one thing it's another.' I was thinking of Ian himself, and how for years I was put off the Catholic Church because he was a member, and carping exponent, of it.

'I said in my letter,' Ian continued, 'it is time these dangerous impurities were purged –'

After that I seldom argued with Ian lest he should win the argument. He could support himself with a range of theological reference unknown to me, and which I simply did not trust him to handle rightly. Moreover, he was a Catholic by birth, and I but a convert; those hereditary Catholics cannot bear to be opposed by newcomers. And again, perhaps most important, I was partly afraid of Ian Brodie, obscurely endangered by him.

Agnes had told me once that her husband was sexually impotent. She had no right to tell me any such thing, but I felt she was not telling me anything that I did not really already know. To this day, I vaguely feel that Ian's impotence is in some way bound up with his suspicions of the Blessed Virgin, which he termed jealousy for the True Faith – a phrase which I noticed Robinson had used in his publication.

During these first weeks on the island I was increasingly struck by similarities between Robinson and Ian Brodie. At the time I exaggerated them, but still, tenuously, they existed. Robinson, short, muscular, and dark-skinned, did not at casual sight look anything like long seedy Ian Brodie; only a likeness between the shape of their heads came to me at odd times. But Robinson was far more intelligent and more controlled.

Again, Robinson's anti-Marian fervour was far more interesting to me than Ian's, for with Robinson it was an obsession of such size that he had left the Church because of it; he had formed for himself a system bound by a simple chain of identities: Mariology was identified with Earth mythology, both were identified with superstition, and superstition with evil. Sterile notion as it seemed to me, still it was a system and he had written it up in his book. Ian Brodie, on the other hand, was dark with inarticulate emotions about religion, which his spasmodic rationalizations failed to satisfy; he was mean by temperament, was a miserable minimist, and was for ever demonstrating how far he could go against the Church without being excommunicated.

And whereas I could never really dislike Robinson, I hated Ian Brodie's guts.

But when Robinson showed his anxiety to keep authority on his island, to know what was going on between us, to prevent our quarrelling or behaving other than impersonally, and to prevent our making friends with Miguel, and, most of all, to detect any possibility of a love affair between Jimmie and me, I was reminded of Ian Brodie, and noticed very much the shape of Robinson's head. I was reminded of instances of Ian Brodie's extraordinary urge to ferret into my private life, and in particular of a morning towards the end of the Easter holidays when I said to my son Brian, 'Let's get out of this.' I telephoned to Agnes, who had arranged to come to tea next day, to tell her I was going abroad for a couple of days.

We went to Dieppe, then caught a bus to Rouen. I was sitting alone outside a café looking at a tower with a big clock, Brian having gone for a walk round about. I half-noticed an English car passing. I was feeling too agreeable with life to be on the alert for anything whatsoever. The car passed again. Brian returned to announce he had found a pastry-cook's owned by a man by the name of Marcel Proust, and this seemed to us both excessively funny. The English car passed again. I saw immediately that it was Ian Brodie's Singer, and that Ian was driving.

'I thought he was in Germany,' said Brian. So did I think he was in Germany. I felt sure he had followed us. I was wrong, but he deserved to be the victim of my suspicions, because of the suspicious way he was driving round and round, past the café where I had been sitting alone. I was not wrong in this, that having caught sight of me alone in Rouen, he had determined to find out who my companion was. He was always inexhaustible in trying to catch me in an illicit love affair, but he never succeeded; and whether this was because I never, in fact, had a lover, or whether I had, but effectively concealed the fact, you may be sure Ian Brodie is still guessing. It was my plan, from the time I became aware of his absorption in this question, to keep him guessing; and always, should his horrible curiosity about my private life appear to flag, I revived it quickly by some careful chance reference which, on his greedy investigation, led him nowhere.

That time in Rouen, when he had noticed that we

had recognized him, it was too late for him to stop with any show of innocence. However, in about ten minutes he passed again, this time going through the motions of recognition.

'I could hardly believe my eyes. What are you doing here?' I should have replied, 'What are *you* doing here?' But I said, 'Oh, just looking round,' while Brian said, 'Taking the air.'

'Oh,' he said, looking from one to the other of us. 'Well, no wonder you're always hard up.'

'Will you have some coffee?' said Brian.

Robinson appeared on the patio carrying three packing cases bound together by string. I shut my notebook guiltily; he noticed this, and I thought, now he has guessed that I've been writing about him. I was coming to terms with this slightly disturbing thought, when he said,

'I ought to have a mule. I've always resisted having a mule because the nuisance of keeping animals on the island sometimes exceeds their usefulness.' I wondered if this was some obscure reference to me, then immediately decided it wasn't. Sometimes I had to resist a tendency to read deep nasty meanings into Robinson's words.

'A mule would be useful for crossing the mountain,' I observed.

'Exactly,' said Robinson. 'I have to take all these packages over the mountain on foot.'

Jimmie came round from the storehouse with two bundles of cartons. They seemed to be heavy.

Tom Wells emerged from the house in his braces, stretching his arms and yawning. 'What's afoot?' he said.

Jimmie pointed to the cartons. 'Is commodities gone to rot.'

'Which, what?' said Wells. He had obviously been deeply sleeping.

Robinson said, 'A certain amount of my tinned food is inconsumable. It has to be disposed of quickly.'

'We open these big tins,' said Jimmie, 'we look, we look away; we look again, and look away.'

There were high stacks of tinned food in the storehouse, great six-pounders as well as the small grocer's-shop kind.

'What about the rest of them?' I said.

'They are all right,' said Robinson. 'It is only part of the last consignment that is damaged.'

Jimmie, anxious to console him, said, 'We dump them in the ocean.'

'We dump them in the Furnace,' said Robinson wearily, 'and I wish I had a mule.'

'Look,' said Wells, 'you don't want to cart that muck over the mountain.'

I said, 'Chuck them over the cliff, then follow them down to the sea.'

'Chuck them over the cliff and keep following them down,' said Jimmie.

'They must go into the Furnace,' said Robinson. 'The food is bad. The tins are opened. The sea will throw them up again, and I can't have my beach littered with rank meat. The Furnace is final.'

'The sharks will demolish them,' I said.

'Not in tins,' said Robinson. 'They draw the line at tins.'

It seemed to me that Robinson was particularly perverse. He heaved the first pack on to his shoulder by its rope and set off for the mountain. Jimmie wanted to accompany him. Robinson firmly refused his help. 'Be a decent chap and stack up the stuff in the store. Put down plenty of disinfectant. The place stinks.'

The smell of the two remaining packs of cartons was fairly fierce. I prepared to accompany Jimmie to the storehouse with buckets of Jeyes' Fluid, while Tom Wells clutched his ribs. 'I hope all the rest of the food is in good condition. There's five weeks to go. We could easily starve,' he said.

'Is in good condition,' said Jimmie; 'we have put to the test the samples of all commodities.'

An hour later Robinson returned for the next package. He looked terribly exhausted. So were Jimmie and I after our exertions in the storehouse. I had made tea, thinking meanwhile at least Tom Wells could have done as much. We sat floppily in the big stone kitchen.

'You've put sugar in my tea,' said Wells. 'I don't take sugar.'

I had done it deliberately. I said:

'Oh, I'll pour another cup for you.'

This I made very watery, but he did not complain about it. However, he said, 'I'm sick and tired of drinking tea without milk.' Our tinned milk was running low.

I said, 'We ought to have lemons. Lemon tea is nice. I am sure lemons could be cultivated here.'

'They couldn't,' said Robinson.

I thought. 'Not if the job was left to you', for the lack of cultivation on the island was a continual irritation to me. It was not simply that it offended some instinct for economy and reproduction. It was more; it offended my aesthetic sense. If you choose the sort of life which has no conventional pattern you have to try to make an art of it, or it is a mess.

I said, 'I think lemons would grow at the foot of the slopes on the South Arm.'

No one paid attention to this remark.

'What with the lack of make-up and the tinned food,' I said, 'my skin is getting very dry.'

'Lemon wouldn't help that condition,' Robinson said.

'Here we are,' said Wells, looking round with a flourish, 'wrecked on a desert island, and January harps about her skin.'

'Is my intention,' said Jimmie to Wells, 'to cast this

84

beverage upon your face in the event that you do not keep your bloody hair on. Is monstrous to declare such offensive insults when a lady is in plight with regard to her complexion on an island.'

Robinson got up. 'Two more trips,' he said.

'Leave them till tomorrow,' said Wells.

'I can't leave them stinking out there on the patio.'

'Dump them on the mountainside for tonight,' I said. 'No need to trek all that way to the Furnace.'

And Jimmie pointed out, in support, 'The mist descends.'

'All right,' said Robinson surprisingly, for he hardly ever accepted any of our advice.

This time he also accepted Jimmie's help in carrying the heavy weights to the mountainside. As they set off I noticed again a look of exhaustion in Robinson, not only in his face but in the droop of his arms and the way he carried himself.

Next day Robinson and Jimmie set off to pick up the packages they had left a short distance up the mountain and carry them to the crater. This was Jimmie's first visit to the Furnace.

'They scream,' he said to me, on his return. 'We have shoved these stinking bundles into the crater. First they roll, then they run, and lo! when they enter this cauldron, is a scream.'

Mr Wells, who had overheard him, said, 'You know, old chap, being stuck on this island is bound to have a psychological effect on one. I feel it myself. It isn't natural to live alone with Nature. I should guard against hallucinations, if I were you. A course of meditation –'

'The Furnace does scream when you throw anything into it,' I said.

Jimmie said to him, 'I like to see you descend into that mighty Furnace. Then is two screams – one is of the Furnace and one is of Mr Wells.'

. . . . . .

In the evenings, however, we did not bicker quite so much. The evening after turning out the storehouse, when we were settled in Robinson's room, some drinking rum, some brandy, we were tired and relaxed with each other so far as to speculate how it would be when we were rescued, how surprised everyone would be.

'I hope to God my wife's gone over to her sister's,' said Wells. 'There's a brother of mine, he's a bachelor, he fancies my wife. I shouldn't be surprised if they haven't got married, me presumed dead. If so, that's just too bad, I'm still the husband – what d'you say, Robinson?'

'You are still the husband,' Robinson said, 'and in any case I think you can't be presumed dead till after seven years.' He spoke very slowly, for he was worn out after his two mountain journeys.

'Is definite that you remain the husband of the wife,' said Jimmie amiably, 'and in the event your brother is an honourable type of bastard, he will not marry your wife. In the contrary event, is manifest that you are bound to black that rotter his eye.'

'I reckon I might do him in,' mused Wells.

'Is to go too far,' said Jimmie. 'No, no. Is better to disfigure his countenance. Is only justice to your wife.'

'I'd give *her* a piece of my mind,' said Wells.

'No, no, please,' said Jimmie. 'Is not nice to give a lady a piece of your mind.'

'Ah well, we're lucky to be alive.'

'The goat must go,' Robinson said.

'Poor Bella, is she very sick?'

'Yes, and suffering.'

'You kill her?' said Jimmie.

'Oh yes, I'll have to shoot her.'

'Is better to slay such a beast with a knife,' said Jimmie.

'Not better,' said Robinson, 'only more traditional.'

'I miss the milk,' said Wells. 'I must say, just as I was getting used to it.'

'Yes, we do miss the milk.'

'Ah well, we're lucky to be alive.'

I recall that evening as the most pleasant few hours I spent on the island. A heavy rainstorm had left the atmosphere moist and cool. Robinson talked, as he sometimes did, of the history and legends of the island. It was a traditional hermits' home. In the fourteenth century, five hermits living on different parts of the island had been attacked by a band of pirates, only one surviving to tell the tale. The island had always been privately owned. It had passed through the hands of a line of Portuguese. Vasco da Gama, on one of his voyages, put in at the island between the North Arm and the North Leg, at a point which was now called Vasco da Gama's Bay. Pirates and smugglers used the island considerably, often without the knowledge of the inhabitants, for there was a cave in the sheer cliffs of the South Arm known as the Market, which was accessible only from the sea, and even then was dangerous to approach, owing to the numerous rocks and a particular whirlpool at its mouth. At the Market, however, the pirates would meet and barter their plunder, so it was said.

From a long crack in the wall of Robinson's room the flying ants were squirming out, spreading their wings and fluttering about. Tom Wells had fallen asleep. I, too, was giving but a drowsy ear to Robinson's voice. I had taken a red cashmere tablecloth from a drawer in the dining-room to use as a shawl which I wore as an Indian sari pinned up over a shirt borrowed from Robinson. This enabled me to wash and repair my shabby green dress, and the change of dress in a way contributed to my peace of mind.

Robinson and Jimmie were arranging to examine a disused ship's boat which lay at the West Leg Bay, with a view to repairing it.

I was so reluctant to disrupt our peace that I put off telling Robinson I had found one of my possessions which I thought had been lost at the time of the crash.

This possession was my rosary. It had been in the pocket of my coat at the time of the crash, and later, when I had recovered, I was not really surprised to have lost it, for although the other contents of the pocket were intact – a handkerchief and a packet of matches – these were comparatively light, and less likely to fly out of my pocket when I was thrown clear of the plane than was my rosary.

I found the rosary in a drawer in Robinson's desk.

I had once casually mentioned to Robinson that my rosary might be somewhere in the vicinity of the wreck, where the salvage had been picked up. 'An antique one,' I said, 'made of rosewood and silver, quite valuable.' Even then I must have sensed that he would be best induced to hand over the rosary if he thought I valued it mainly for its antiquity, rosewood and silver. And it was indeed a very attractive object.

I found it quite unexpectedly in Robinson's desk. It is true I had no business to open the drawers and examine his papers and read the letters. I suppose I desired to find out to what extent he resembled Ian Brodie, and I suppose I hoped to discover something bearing on his relationship with Jimmie and his family: so far I had only Jimmie's version, which was most engaging, and invited further investigation. Anyway, I went to his desk in the first place to borrow the pencil-sharpener, and was waylaid by curiosity. And anyway, I found my rosary at the back of the second right-hand drawer. I took it away with me and lest I should judge Robinson too hard I also took a cigarette.

Two days later I was busy in the kitchen preparing to cook some nettles I had got Jimmie to gather. I had remembered reading about the vitamin properties of nettles, and I felt our diet needed improvement.

From the open lattice I saw Robinson leading the very sick goat from its pen. It occurred to me he might kill the goat there in front of the window.

I called out, 'Robinson! Don't kill it here. I can't bear the sight of blood.'

'I'm going to take her up the mountain near the Furnace,' he said.

A picture of Bella's corpse sliding into the Furnace and screaming came to my mind. I ran out and stroked the creature which stood in a weary stupor. Miguel ran up and hugged her, almost knocking her down, for she was thin and frail.

Miguel was crying.

I said, 'Never mind, Miguel. I have something to show you.'

Robinson said quickly, 'If you mean the rosary, I do not want the boy to see it.'

Miguel looked interested. 'Show me Rosie.'

This was the first sign that Robinson had discovered the absence of the rosary from his desk.

'I intended to tell you that I had found it,' I said.

'What's it like?' said Miguel.

'Rather nice. Silver and rosewood.'

'Show me Rosewood,' said Miguel.

'I simply don't want the child to see it,' Robinson said. 'He's extremely susceptible to that sort of thing.'

I stroked poor Bella, and tried to interest her in her bucket of water, but she would not touch it.

'That sort of thing can easily corrupt the Faith,' Robinson said.

'What bloody rot,' I said with a vehemence intended more for Ian Brodie than for Robinson. 'What a fuss to make about a rosary.'

'Let's see the rosary,' said Miguel.

Robinson led the drooping goat away through the gate to the mountain path. Miguel followed him, but he was sent back within twenty minutes.

'Robinson wouldn't let me stop and watch Bella die.'

'Robinson is quite right,' I said snappily.

'Show me –'

'Make yourself scarce for half an hour, because I'm busy,' I said.

The sound of a shot bounded down from the mountain.

'Poor old Bella,' said Miguel. 'Will she be dead now?'

'Yes.'

'Perhaps she won't die first shot.'

'Robinson's a careful shot,' I said.

'Will there be blood?'

'Not much.'

Ian Brodie used to return from the Continent having gone out of his way to feed his fury by witnessing all the religious processions and festivals.

'Awful old crones hobbling along after the statues, clinking their rosaries, mumbling their Hail Marys, as if their lives depended on it. And the sickening thing, young people, people in their prime, caught up in the mob hysteria. That sort of thing corrupts the Faith.' Ian Brodie would almost foam at the mouth in these denunciations. And sometimes, both repelled and attracted, I could not keep my eyes off him – Ian, mouthing his contempt, looked positively lustful.

'Why do you go near the shrines? Why do you watch the festivals if they upset you?' I said. 'Surely you must be tired of being so upset.'

'You can't avoid them in Italy,' he said.

'Why not go to Iceland for your holidays?' I said.

'You would find them there,' spluttered Ian. 'You find these fanatics everywhere.'

'That's true,' I said, looking hard at him.

'You never seem to realize the materialistic implication of all these demonstrations,' said Ian. 'You don't understand the gravity of what's going on in those orgies and processions you go in for.'

'I don't go in for them,' I said.

'All this Mariolatry is eating the Christian heart out of the Catholic faith,' said Ian. 'It is a materialistic heresy.'

'What bloody rot,' I said. And if there was one thing against which I did feel strongly at that moment, it was Ian Brodie, with his offensive way of looking at a woman. I thought: no wonder Agnes vows she will never become a Catholic.

I held Ian in such contempt that from time to time I wished to do him a wrong, and to rid myself of the self-righteous feelings he provoked. My most effective method of hurting Ian was to tell him that I had won money on a horse, even if I hadn't. This served to injure him in two ways: one, he was reminded that he had no influence over me – for he was morally against betting; and two, the mere suggestion that anyone but himself had received a sum of money, let alone money for nothing, really upset him, really gave him a pain.

Looking forward to going home, I was necessarily looking backward. Ian Brodie had been loud against me leaving home for so long a period. Brian went away to school; he liked the idea. Therefore so did I. And I thought it would be good for him to have a change from Curly Lonsdale's company. Ian Brodie's suspicion was that I had a lover whom I proposed to meet abroad, in term-time, returning prim and replenished to my chaste widowhood for the summer holidays: I was indebted to Agnes for this information.

Looking forward to my going home, my return from the dead, my intrusion into whatever new arrangements had been made, I had often in mind my past encounters with

Ian. I liked to picture the effect if I arrived with Jimmie in my wake. For Jimmie was always saying, 'If I give my candid opinion, is providential that you are not consumed in the aeroplane so as to marry me.'

Ian usually got into a state of horrible excitement if he had cause to suspect that I might get married. At the same time as I let my mind wander round the possibilities of Jimmie – possibilities like his threatening to black Ian's eye – I was calculating the price of this tempting form of entertainment. And when I tell you that I have another category of acquaintance, certain dry-eyed poets and drifters dear to my heart, you may see the extent of my temptation in the matter of accepting Jimmie. For many a time did I sit on the banks of the blue and green lake reflecting how highly these intelligent loafers, whose regard I valued, would regard me, should I fetch into captivity so exceptional and well-spoken a bird as Jimmie. They would have him along to Soho. They would have delight for at least half a year.

Journal, Thursday, 1st July – Jimmie Waterford was born in 1919. He is a second cousin of Robinson, having been brought up in Gibraltar by Robinson's mother, his father being dead, his mother having disappeared.

The circumstances of Jimmie's mother's disappearance were this. Soon after her widowhood she went on a visit to her parents in Namur, leaving Jimmie with his nurse in Holland. In her father's household was a chef of whom he was very proud. He set so much store by his chef's cooking that he would not permit his family to season their food according to taste. Few guests came to his table, lest they should require salt and pepper, and then only those who understood and acquiesced in their host's rule, for this father held that the food was excellent without additional seasoning, but with it all would be ruined, the chef insulted.

Invariably, however, the ancient silver cruets were caused to appear on the table, for form's sake. Regularly, they were emptied and refilled, any laxity in this respect being a high domestic crime.

On the first evening of her visit, Jimmie's mother casually reached for the great heavy salt, and ignoring the choking cries which proceeded from her father's throat, ignoring his bulging eyes and her mother's fluttering hands, she placed a little salt on the side of her plate. The father turned her out of the house that very hour. She was not impoverished, she went to an inn for the night, and might well have returned to her home in the north of Holland the next day. But the being turned out on the streets with all her baggage seemed to give her the idea, and she remained on the streets for the rest of her known life.

To this day, I don't know whether this particular story is true. There was just enough of the element of rootless European frivolity in Jimmie to make any yarn about his connexions seem possible, or, on the other hand, to make suspect his stories; and this may have been part of his wooing, he may have sensed that I am a pushover for a story, that I would far rather have a present of a good story than, say, a bunch of flowers, and will more or less always take kindly to the raconteur type.

I was able to substantiate some of his tales later on, when I found the evidence among Robinson's papers. Certainly he was related to Robinson and had been brought up in Gibraltar by Robinson's mother. I think it possible that Jimmie was an illegitimate child of Robinson's father, and so a half-brother to Robinson. The facts he had given me concerning Robinson were apparently correct, for I found letters addressed to Mexico, and many touching on the theological problems which had engaged him then, and on the question of his leaving the Church. But where Jimmie himself was concerned, his life and adventures, I doubted as much as I was amused.

When, up to our seventh week on the island, he sat beside me in the afternoons, between the blue and green lake and the mustard field, and embarked on his memories: 'Along about the time that the hostilities were declared . . .' I felt sure that Jimmie was the most delightful man I had ever met, not in the least without wondering whether he had, in fact, taken such a part in the Resistance, had escaped with a pair of Gestapo trousers as a memento, had rescued the Polish countess – she in the hollow sideboard, he disguised as a furniture remover. About these and other exploits I shall never quite know. Of course, it is possible they are true; I myself once attended the Derby disguised as a gipsy, and there waylaid Ian Brodie who refused to cross my palm with silver, though I importuned him somewhat, he being present not to bet or to watch the races, but on business which he called sociological research – in reality to lacerate himself with the loathsome spectacle of an hysterical nation. I got away with it: Ian never knew that I know what he is like when solicited by a gipsy. And so perhaps I am wrong to doubt the adventures of Jimmie.

Later that day I added to my journal of 1st July:

The uncle who was entrusted with Robinson's future died at the beginning of this year. The money is mostly in the motor-scooter business, and one of the reasons for Jimmie's concern about it is this. He is the next beneficiary after Robinson, and is Robinson's heir. So far Robinson has been indifferent to Jimmie's arguments, refuses to return, or in any way to consolidate the motor-scooter concern.

Tom Wells is still making a fuss about the papers which he says are missing from his case. He has even been the the scene of the crash to search for them. He swears that he saw the papers in his bag in the plane just before the crash. Robinson maintains that the papers could not have escaped from the bag, since it was firmly shut when he found it.

The next day, Friday, the second of July, I discovered that my rosary was missing again, from the pocket of my coat where I had put it. For the rosary devotion a chain of rosary beads is not strictly necessary, you can say the rosary on your fingers. The reasons for my distress were, one, that it was my only material possession apart from the clothes I had been wearing at the time of the accident; two, although you can say the rosary on your fingers, there is nothing quite like the actual thing; three, this was a beautiful object, unique and, unlike my clothes, intact; four, I had intended to show it to Miguel, and so win his attention; five, and most pressing, to lose my rosary so soon after having found it gave me a sense of fatal misgiving, and I realized that I had attached to its discovery an important mystique. Then there was a sixth reason, the mystery of its disappearance. Last thing at night it had been in the pocket of my coat hanging up behind the door of my room. First thing in the morning it had gone. The rosary had been removed from my pocket during the night. I decided to make a fuss, and went to look for Robinson.

He had left the house, and there was no sign either of Jimmie or Miguel. I remembered then that they had arranged to leave early on their expedition to the West Leg Bay to examine the old ship's boat.

I found Tom Wells out on the patio shaving, a sight which usually I could not bear. Tom Wells would wash and dress all over the house and grounds, rubbing his face with a towel as he walked along the corridors, putting on his shirt as he came into breakfast; and although I think Robinson did not like it, he put up with it.

As I approached, Wells said, 'Pardon me shaving out here. The light's better.'

I said, 'Have you seen my rosary? I've lost it.'

'Pardon?'

I repeated my question.

He said, 'Didn't know you had a rosary. What's it like?'

I said, 'A chain of rosewood beads with a silver crucifix at the end.'

He said, 'Oh, one of those R.C. items.'

'Have you seen it anywhere?'

'No, lovey.'

'It was in the pocket of my coat last night. This morning it was gone.'

He said, 'I heard Robinson up and about during the night. They all left early.'

'If Robinson has taken it,' I said, 'I'll murder him.'

'Could be Robinson,' he said. 'He's R.C., isn't he?'

'I don't know about that,' I said. 'The point is, he has no right to take my possessions.'

'True enough,' said Wells. He put away the shaving things neatly in Robinson's fitted box. 'And I should like to know what's happened to my papers. Now listen, while we're on the subject, dear. I want to talk to you.'

'I must look for my rosary,' I said. 'I must make sure I haven't dropped it somewhere.' I was still prepared to make a fuss.

'Wait a minute, dear.'

'You're ready for breakfast,' I said. 'I'll go and make the coffee.'

But, over our coffee with tinned milk and hard biscuits, he said, 'What d'you make of Robinson?'

'If I find that he came to my room while I was asleep and took my rosary there will be hell to pay.'

Wells laughed. 'He wouldn't come to your room for anything else, my dear, I can tell you that much. He's not a lady's man, I can tell you.'

'Oh, I was not suggesting –'

'I bet you aren't. There's your boy-friend too. *He's* another.'

'Another?'

'Queer.'

'What?'

'Homosexuals, both of them. Disgusting. Unnatural.' He

pushed away his plate violently as if that too were disgusting and unnatural.

I have come across men before who imagine that every other man who does not rapidly make physical contact with his female prey is a homosexual. And some who I know regard all celibates as homosexuals.

'Mind you,' said Tom Wells, 'your boy-friend has looks, I don't deny. And of course I don't deny that Robinson is a fine chap in his way. To hear him talk is an education in itself. But what I'm telling you is for your own sake, sweetie; these homos can be spiteful, so just watch yourself.'

I said, 'I prefer not to discuss the subject, for I don't think you understand it.' I did not at all feel that I could convey the temperamental shades of Robinson and Jimmie to Tom Wells. I did not feel called to do so.

It was true that sometimes a sort of tendresse was evident between them, that Jimmie would crinkle between his third and index finger the light waves of his hair, that Robinson was not 'a lady's man'. I felt incapable of convincing Tom Wells that such things were not conclusive, not even unusual in men. For he would have repeated, as I had heard Curly Lonsdale say, 'Do you think *I* don't know a man when I see one?' – as if the whole world consisted of the class of society with which they were familiar. But in any case I did not feel obliged to explain anything to Tom Wells. 'In any case,' I said, 'it is not our business.'

But Tom Wells gave me a look that might be described as 'knowing' except for the fact that it was also calculating. He winked knowingly at me, and I detected the calculation in the other eye. It was at this moment that the idea first came to me that Wells was a blackmailer. I had no clear reason for retaining the idea, but certain propositions came clearly to my mind. One, it was probable that Wells be-believed a homosexual relationship to exist between Robinson and Jimmie; two, whether this was true or not was irrelevant to Wells; three, his purpose in speaking of it to me was not, as he had said, to warn me, but to establish it as a fact in my mind; four, he was capable of saying anything about anyone if it served his own ends.

Miguel came rushing in dangling a dead hare by its ears. He ran to show it to Tom Wells, his enchanter.

I inquired of Robinson that afternoon about my rosary. He neither admitted nor denied having taken it.

'If you came into my room while I was asleep and searched my pocket, that was very wrong,' I said, using my best moral tone, since, after all, he set himself up as our moral organizer.

'Whose room?' he said.

'Mine,' I said.

'Really?' he said. 'Yours?'

I could tell by this rather mean defence that Robinson felt himself to be in the wrong.

'I should like to have my rosary,' I said.

'Will you promise not to teach Miguel to recite it?'

'I'll promise nothing. Give me my property.'

'I am thinking of Miguel,' he said. 'I wish him to grow up free from superstition.'

'To hell with you,' I said. 'There's nothing superstitious about the rosary. It's a Christian devotion, not a magic charm.'

'All those Hail Marys,' he said.

I realized suddenly that Robinson was not speaking in the normal course of argument, not stating his objections to my request, or putting his point of view against mine. He knew very well the contents of the rosary meditations, and he was probably less ignorant of their nature than I was. It struck me for the first time that he was not simply attempting to make small difficulties, or to exercise his authority on the island simply from a need for power, but that he was constitutionally afraid of any material manifestation of Grace.

'Oh well,' I said, 'I can do without it.'

I was not surprised that, late that night when I was going to bed, Tom Wells stood in my path to tell me that his brief-case containing his samples of lucky charms, all his proofs of *Your Future*, and the articles he had been writing, had disappeared.

Chapter 8

NEXT morning, Saturday the third of July, Robinson was
gone. It was nothing for him to have gone out before the
rest of us were up, but he had always returned before eleven
o'clock. We had breakfast and proceeded with our usual
chores. At noon we asked each other where Robinson could
be. At one o'clock Miguel began to cry.

Robinson's bed was made, his room in order. He was
nowhere in the house. He was not in the storehouse, nor in
that vicinity. We assembled at the cliff's edge calling,
'Robinson! Hey there, Robinson!' lest he should be down
on the beach, or have fallen.

We gave Miguel some soup, feeding him by spoonfuls, for
he was sobbing frantically. Jimmie and I, taking with us
some chunky biscuit-sandwiches and the first-aid box, set
off to look for Robinson, for it seemed certain that he had
met with some accident. We took a route over the mountain
to the north-west since this was a part scored with the
streams rich in iron deposits, from which Robinson frequently drew our mineral water supplies in the early mornings. Tom Wells remained with Miguel, promising to keep
a look-out for Robinson from the plateau.

We had gone a short way when Miguel climbed up behind
us, calling on us to stop. 'Come back now! Come back.' He
had stopped crying. He looked suddenly like an old man
who had started growing downward with age, or again like
a child of the very poor, with a face lined with responsibility
and want.

'Has Robinson turned up?'

'No. Mr Tom has found the blood.'

'Robinson must be hurt,' I said.

We returned, Jimmie carrying Miguel astride on his shoulders, and Miguel hunched and clinging to him.

Tom Wells came to meet us. He held out towards us a heavy corduroy jacket of a faded tawny colour, which I recognized as one of Robinson's which he would sometimes wear when the weather turned cold, or if he went out of doors at night.

'We found this in the mustard field,' Tom Wells said

'What is with Robinson?' said Jimmie.

'Look at the coat.'

I saw a bright red stain on the coat. I felt it. The stain was damp, it was sticky with blood, and it spread across three separate gashes in the material.

Jimmie exclaimed some words in Dutch.

I said, 'Someone must be hurt.'

'It was lying in the mustard field,' said Wells. 'Miguel lifted it up, and this knife fell out of the pocket.' He reached in the pocket of the coat and produced a clasp-knife. The blade was open. I recognized the knife. It was very sharp, the handle about three inches long, the blade about four inches. Robinson always carried it with him, clasped in its sheath.

I said, 'That's Robinson's knife.'

We went down to the mustard field, and there, even before Miguel ran to point out the spot where the coat had been found, I saw the dark trampled patches among the glaring yellow plants. There was blood on the ground, still slightly sticky. When we came to look closer, there seemed to be the marks of blood all round about. There was also a complete pathway of trodden-down plants spattered with blood, leading out of the field from the spot where the coat had been found. Following this newly-beaten track, towards the mountain path, we found a green silk neck square which was Jimmie's property. This was also soaked in blood, not yet dry.

Jimmie opened our pack and brought out the brandy. This he solemnly handed round. We all had a swig, even Miguel.

Tom Wells said, 'There's something fishy about all this. Someone wounded has been dragged through the field, you realize.'

I lay awake all night, listening to Robinson's elegant eight-day clock chiming the hours. It occurred to me obscurely that I had better wind it in the morning, otherwise we would be without a time-measure on the island. Winding this clock was of course Robinson's concern, and Robinson was gone. But the thought was absurd, muscling its way in among the major disturbances of my mind. For the turmoil and the frightened talk and conjecture, the strangeness and dread of the past day crowded in, almost as if I had a capacity prepared for it; as if, from the time of the crash up to this day I had been a vacuum waiting only for the swift delayed rush of horror to enter in; as if, really, the getting away with a mere concussion and a broken arm, my luck in falling into Robinson's hands, my easy recovery, and the normal life of Robinson's household, were not to have been trusted; and as if the proper consequence of the plane disaster were now upon us. From among the shapes and shadows of the past day I discerned several hard outlines: the trail from the mustard field had led to the mountain. Here, a path linked up with that which crossed the mountain to the Furnace. Now that we were definitely looking for blood, we saw blood smeared everywhere along the trail. There must have been a steady bleeding, a dropping of blood all the way. Moreover at various stations we came across blood-stained articles either on the actual track or nearby: a shoe belonging to Robinson, a shirt – the one I had been wearing on the previous day while my dress was being washed, and, a little farther up the path, the scarlet cashmere tablecloth which I had worn as a sari. These I had laid aside the previous night, and, putting on my newly washed dress in the morning, had not noticed their absence from my room. The white cotton shirt was streaked with blood which had almost dried and on the red cashmere was a patch of darker red which stained the whole of one side down to the fringe and which, in places, was still sticky. Tom Wells, who had picked it up from the thick plants a few yards off the pathway, pulled his hand away quickly as it touched the sticky patches. I noticed that he did this every time his hand encountered blood not yet dry. I thought this gesture odd, until I noticed that I myself gave the same involuntary jerk of withdrawal when my hand touched wet blood. After stopping to look stupidly at each of these objects, we left them lying on the track and pushed on like somnambulists.

Half-way to the Furnace, at the point where we had sight of the sea on both sides, Tom Wells clutched his ribs and said he could go no farther.

'Go back,' I said, 'and take Miguel with you.'

'No, I'm coming after Robinson,' Miguel said.

'Come with Mr Tom,' said Tom Wells.

'I want Robinson.' He was beside himself, both younger and ages older than his years.

Jimmie and I pressed on while Miguel went fitfully ahead looking from right to left, and behind him to see if we still followed.

At some point I said, 'I wonder, would there be another inhabitant of the island – someone we don't know about?'

'Is possible,' said Jimmie.

He gave me a hand up the steep places, automatically, not with his usual deliberate air.

'It seems that Robinson has been attacked. At least someone has been attacked,' I said.

'Excuse me,' said Jimmie, 'that I do not converse, as I lose my nerves.'

We found other blood-stained articles on which the blood had dried in the heat of the afternoon. We found a small pocket handkerchief – it was mine, it had been in my pocket at the time of the crash; we found a blue silk vest which Jimmie had been wearing at the time of the crash; the other of Robinson's shoes; and lastly, at the head of the dip leading to the Furnace, we saw more of Robinson's clothes, another jacket of his, dark tweed, his brown corduroy trousers, his underclothes. These were scattered bloodily down the slope that ran into the gurgling crater, and a clear streak of torn-up vegetation, revealing the raw red earth as if there had been a landslide, completed the run from the rim of the crater to its mouth. The volcano chuckled, and gave out its red vapours, as if that too were a sort of blood. I thought of the crater's scream, and I screamed. Jimmie limply placed the brandy to my lips.

I had all this blood before my eyes as I lay awake, trying to isolate the details of the day. On the journey back we had found other things: a blood-stained scarf which Robinson always wore against the mist; his fountain-pen, his pocket compass.

I did not remember if or how we had eaten that day, nor do I remember this even now, except that we gave Miguel a sedative tablet with warm milk, and that he was asleep before the sun had set.

I recalled, too, there had been some talk between Tom Wells and me. Jimmie had gone out in his stunned silence and was roaming about the beach at the Pomegranate Bay. All I recall of my conversation that evening with Wells was the following:

I said, 'Those blood-stained articles of clothing must have been planted by someone.'

'Oh, must they?'

'They would not be scattered about in quite such an obvious manner if they had been dropped accidentally.'

'Oh, wouldn't they?'

I could not put out of my mind the blood. Even when I closed my eyes it was like a red light penetrating the lids. And when I tried to recall the past day, I had the rare and distressing experience of becoming objectively conscious of my rational mind in action, separate from all others, as one might see the open workings of a clock. This only happens to me when faced with a group of facts which hurt my reasoning powers – as one becomes highly conscious of a limb when it is damaged.

But having set my mind painfully to arrange the facts, I immediately got out of bed and, slipping my coat over my borrowed pyjamas, padded bare-foot along the corridors to Robinson's rooms, aided only by the moon sidling in through the narrow slit windows. There I found Robinson's bunch of house keys hanging in their usual place. At the same time I fumbled among the pigeon-holes in his desk until I found a small electric torch which he usually kept there. I used the torch, since I did not know my way very well, to guide me up a flight of two or three shallow steps, round a stone-flagged bend, and along another corridor to the gun-room. There, without bothering to light the lamp which stood ready with its box of matches, I tried one key after another in the door until I had found the right one. With the help of the torch I extracted this key from the bunch, and locked the door. I returned the bunch of keys to its peg in Robinson's room, keeping the gun-room key for myself. I went next to the kitchen where string was kept in a drawer. Here in the kitchen my whole body shook as I thought, with a new realization, of Robinson and what could have befallen him. However, I cut myself a length of string, and with this tied the gun-room key round my neck.

I snapped out the torch and returned to my room, led by the moonlit window slits. As I passed Jimmie's room I jumped, for instead of the dark shut door there was an open space with Jimmie standing in it, regarding me.

I did not speak to him, but walked on to my room, satisfied that he had only just opened his door having heard the moving about, that he had seen nothing of my performance with the key, and that I had done a reasonable thing, considering that I was on an island with a child and two men, one of them probably a murderer. I had done this, but the small reasonable satisfaction was swallowed up in fear, in the gashes of red on the screen of my mind, and the absurdity of all I had seen, which made me exclaim aloud from time to time throughout the night, 'It can't be so! How *can* it be?' I kept thinking that Robinson was bound to walk in next morning and explain everything, the seriousness of the situation being evident to me then only by my recalling Miguel's distress.

Throughout the next two weeks I lived in a state similar to my first weeks on the island, concussion, stupor. So it appeared. I feared and suspected much. I formed opinions, and wondered sometimes if Robinson's disappearance were a dream or the whole island affair a dream, or life itself, my past life, Brian, Chelsea, were a dream.

We collected the blood-stained clothes from the route. The stains were still sticky, having dried and become moist again from the mists. I piled them up in a heap on the floor of Robinson's bedroom, thinking as I did so that an inquest on Robinson would be held after the boat should come to rescue us with our news.

It took us twelve days to search the island. But already by the third day after Robinson's disappearance we all more or less assented that he was dead.

I thought: either, therefore, he has been killed by Jimmie

or Tom Wells, or by both together. Suffering from head-
aches, I chewed over all other hypotheses – that he had
killed himself, had been murdered by Miguel, or by myself
in my sleep, or by another, unknown inhabitant of the
island; but I rejected these as folly. Again and again I
returned to Jimmie, Tom Wells, or both together. I did
not think it at all likely that they were accomplices, but
I added that possibility to my list for a show of objectivity.

Tom Wells produced a theory of his own, one which I
considered brought him under suspicion for having suggested it. A supernatural force, he declared, had done away
with Robinson, in revenge for some sacrilege done to the
lucky charms which Robinson had confiscated.

'You mean a poltergeist?'

'Something like that.'

There were many difficulties in the way of our searching
the island. Tom Wells pleaded his damaged ribs against the
exertion required of him for the amount of climbing entailed.
And so the task of searching the island fell on Jimmie and
me, with Miguel for our guide. Neither Tom Wells nor
Jimmie seemed to see it as an imperative task, but I insisted
on this course, formality though it might be, so that we should
know as far as possible where we stood.

'Is evidence that he lies in the Furnace,' Jimmie said.

'Still, we must eliminate everything else.'

Tom Wells said, 'There's an evil force on this island.
I think we should stay put here in the house, I've had a
serious time of it with my ribs.'

Now I had resolved, if possible, to avoid being alone with
any one of these men, these strangers. Therefore I had to
go everywhere, in the course of our examination, with
Jimmie and Miguel, rather than stay at the house with Wells.
He complained, 'I don't like the idea of your all going off
from early morning till late at night. I don't like being alone,
quite frankly, after what's happened.'

And then Jimmie's quaintness had altogether lost its charm for me at this time, it exasperated me. And when he declaimed, 'Ah me! Man is born, he suffers, he dies', it sounded to me frivolous, if not false.

Also there was trouble about guns. Jimmie said we must take a gun with us. 'Is only reasonable. We see a stranger, we shoot.'

'Haven't you seen enough blood?' I said. But this was my being afraid, making a diversion while I worked out what could be done.

'The gun-room's locked,' said Tom Wells, 'for some reason which is beyond me.'

I said, 'I have the key.'

'It's time we had a bit of rabbit,' said Wells. 'You'll have to hand over the key. We have to have guns for food.'

I said to Jimmie, 'I'll fetch a gun for you now, if you promise to give it back to me when we return. I want to keep charge of the guns.'

'Is entirely to be understood. Is reasonable,' said Jimmie.

'Look here,' said Wells. 'I don't think a woman should have charge of the guns. I don't agree to that.'

'You will agree,' said Jimmie.

'I hold the key,' I said, or something to that effect, and went to fetch a Winchester rifle for Jimmie, with some cartridges. For myself I chose a baby Browning automatic. I could not find any cartridges. I have a fear of handling guns, and so it was an effort for me to examine the Browning. I found it loaded. I locked the armoury, went to my room to fetch my coat, gave another neurotic look at the safety-catch of the automatic, and, putting it in my pocket, I then felt safe to take the big gun to Jimmie.

This was Tuesday, the sixth of July. That day we explored the South Arm, descending from our mountain to rich downy grassland. We examined the deserted mill and cottage. We walked round the coast, stopped only by the perpendicular cliffs, which stretched for half a mile on the western seafront of the little peninsula. Here, there was no beach nor access by land, the cliffs dropping sheer into the sea.

Trailing along beside Jimmie, I experienced over again the days of concussion when my actions were mechanical, my senses hazy. But then I had been safe. You must understand that Jimmie and Tom Wells had all at once become strangers to me, far more than when I first fell in with them, for now their familiar characteristics struck me merely as a number of indications that I knew nothing about them.

Five times we were lost in a sudden mist, and once it seemed that we should be wandering all night until, with Miguel huddled on Jimmie's shoulder, we found ourselves to be a few yards from home. Usually, we were home before the big night mists fell.

I remember watching my shadow with the sun behind it, making me tall, very tall, but not so tall as Jimmie in his shadow.

By the end of twelve days we had completed our search, having covered the South Arm, the Headland with its neat pomegranate orchards, the rocky North Arm and North Leg, the ferny meadows of the West Leg. We covered the black and white coast-line, with its cliffs and beaches; we gave two days to the central mountain, climbing, trekking, leaping, and I was glad of our exhaustion and the lack of any energy to speak to one another. Usually I followed after Jimmie, but if ever I found myself in front of him I took firm hold of the automatic concealed in my pocket. Miguel was usually some distance ahead of us. On one of these excursions I had said to him, 'I have a little gun in my pocket. If you should hear me fire it, you must run away.' I said this in case he should be hurt in any tussle between Jimmie and me.

These, I thought, were reasonable precautions. All the time I really suspected Tom Wells. And all the time I smoked cigarettes, Robinson's share as well as my own.

My shoes were worn through. I rummaged among the tidy bundles of salvage, for I had no more squeamishness after the sight of so much blood. At last I found a pair of shoes only slightly too big, and a little charred at the toe.

On the eleventh day we rested. On the twelfth day we set out for the subterranean caves. Miguel was at first reluctant to take us. I suppose he felt their secrets were a sort of possession of Robinson.

'It's important, Miguel. Suppose we should find Robinson?'

'Robinson could not live in the caves. They aren't for living in. They're for going through.'

'Someone else may be hiding there.'

'There's no one on the island.'

Miguel was still frightened. We kept telling him that everything would be all right, that we would look after him, that he was our boy. He did not take in this talk. He did not fail to interpret the strangeness, the suspicion, and the fear between us.

At last I had to say to Miguel, 'If you won't take us to the caves we will have to look for them ourselves. We might get lost and never come back.' And so he set off with us on the twelfth day of our search.

There were three tunnels in all, one leading from the Pomegranate Bay in the south to the region of the deserted mill and homestead at the South Arm. A second passage cut through the mountain from the cliff-top behind our plateau, its entrance being a vertical cleft among some thick shrubbery; this led to a point in the mountain approaching the Furnace. The third tunnel started among the lava boulders of the North Arm. This was the longest, and most difficult to negotiate. It emerged at the beach on the east side of Vasco da Gama's Bay.

The first tunnel was the one through which Miguel had given me the slip when I had taken my first walk down to the beach. The entrance was amazingly obvious once it was pointed out. I had passed it several times without noticing how it stood like a slim shadow in the mountain wall, within a fluted grotto. Miguel led the way, then Jimmie. After the narrow mouth the tunnel was about nine feet in width, the height here being about seven feet, although presently Jimmie had to stoop. I began to cough. I said, 'I shall choke.' This was caused by a combination of sulphurous dust, breathless heat and a powerful lava smell. I felt we were walking into the hot centre of the earth. 'I shall choke, choke,' said my echo.

'Please to return and wait for us,' said Jimmie. He too seemed suffocated by the dust and heat. Miguel coughed, but did not seem to mind.

I could not answer Jimmie for coughing, but I intended to agree to his suggestion, when he added, 'Is not suitable conditions for a lady.'

I do not know why, but his phraseology caused me to remember that Jimmie was heir to Robinson's fortunes. And when I had recovered from my fit of coughing, I said, 'I'm coming with you. I wish to satisfy myself that the caves are empty.'

His flashlamp cast a rusty light: I suppose the place was filled with motes of red dust. By this light Miguel's dark skin and lean figure showed up fiendishly. Jimmie's head was in darkness, and I could only see the dim red glow of the man's long body. Very much later, thinking over the scene, it occurred to me that I too must have looked ghoulish in the caves.

A shallow rivulet led to the entrance of the cave, and was flowing feebly beside us. Jimmie turned and squelched his way down into the tunnel. Miguel and I followed. I stopped every few minutes to recover from my coughing.

We came to a point where even Miguel had to stoop very low, and to squeeze round a narrow bend in the rock. Here the stream was deeper, reaching my knees and Miguel's thighs. This narrow passage gave out on to a vast chamber all over which Jimmie directed his torch. The air here was cleaner. I could not see any further opening from this huge cave-room, but Miguel splashed over to the far wall and there he seemed to climb up the wall and melt into it. We followed him to that spot, and found a small shelf behind which lay a gap. We heaved ourselves up and slid through, emerging at the foot of a steep, slippery, black cliff which Miguel had started to climb very skilfully. Several times I had to take the hand which Jimmie held down to help me. At the top we came to daylight, and the tall grasses of the South Arm. We had been in the tunnel about twenty minutes.

I could see that Jimmie did not want to do any more subterranean crawls. Nor would I have been reluctant to put off our ventures into the two remaining tunnels until the next day. But Jimmie did not make any suggestion to this effect – I think because he was convinced I would disagree. And I said nothing, fearing he would think my vigilance was waning. I was not in a condition which could be called vigilant: I was half-doped, my imagination overwhelmed. I could hardly look at the facts, far less piece them together, but I felt bound to impress on Jimmie and Tom Wells that I was capable of doing so.

We returned to the house to wash, for we were covered with rusty grime. Immediately after our meal we set out for the second tunnel, the entrance to which lay near the back of the house. 'Is pity,' said Jimmie, 'that no policeman resides here who should undertake these searchings.' I thought, perhaps it is irony, or perhaps it is only one of his silly remarks.

The second tunnel took fifteen minutes to explore. This too was full of volcanic dust and on the floor throughout lay a lot of slimy weed which made our progress dangerous. When Jimmie called back to me, 'Is dangerous,' the words were repeated again and again on the walls of the cave and its recesses and I listened to the 'dangerous, dangerous', encouraging myself with the thought that although I was outmatched in physical strength by Jimmie and Tom Wells, their joint intelligence was probably not superior to mine. I realized that my sense of danger was enhanced by the loss of Robinson's intelligence. It also occurred to me that Tom Wells, should he become troublesome, would not hesitate to use Miguel as an ally. Miguel was well acquainted with the island. On the other hand he was not clever in the sense that Tom Wells would find cleverness useful.

Towards the end of the second tunnel we had to stoop very low, and to crawl for several yards, the smell of the Furnace increasing as we approached the exit. The cave widened gradually, and still stooping we assisted our progress by clutching at various shelves and protrusions in the walls. The last few steps, and I slipped, grazing my knee. Jimmie heaved me up, and it was not until we were standing outside that he handed me the automatic which, unnoticed by me, had fallen out of my pocket when I fell.

'Thanks, Jimmie,' I said, giving him a sort of pleasant smile.

But he was not deceived; he seemed to expect such tactics from me.

It was impossible to be near the Furnace without being drawn to gaze into it. We walked across to the crater's edge and stood staring into the wide bubbling basin. Jimmie unlodged a rock and shoved it down the slide. It entered the turmoil with a scream. I looked up, and caught him watching my face. It came to me with a shock that he might be testing my reaction to the scream. I had never thought that I myself could be under suspicion. Immediately, of course, I felt myself to be looking guilty, and quickly to cover it I said, 'That scream makes me feel ill', which immediately seemed the wrong thing to say. That I should be thought a potential killer was a large new idea. Nervously, I unloosed a rock substantially bigger than that which Jimmie had thrown in, and I sent it screaming into the Furnace. I suppose my intention was to prove that I was not really afraid of the scream. Jimmie looked at the large patch of earth from which I had heaved the boulder, and remarked, 'You are strong.'

Just then, from the depth of the turbulent mud there came a sudden splutter, followed by a loud sigh. Jimmie looked as startled as I was, but instantly I remembered that Robinson had told me, of the Furnace, 'Sometimes it sighs.'

I said to Jimmie. 'Did you get a fright?'

'Ah, no.'

I said, 'I thought you had lost your nerve.'

He said, 'Is not at this moment that I lose my nerves. Is when I have descended from the skies into this island of sorrows.'

Our last excursion under the mountain took forty minutes. This tunnel we approached by a grotto on the narrow beach of Vasco da Gama's Bay, at the North Arm. The light was so refracted from its walls that one did not see, until one had fairly penetrated the cave, that a flight of steps had been hacked out of the rock, leading into a deep dark pit. It smelt of lime and lava, and a fairly deep stream gurgled along the floors at about twenty feet below sea level. The path along the edge of the river was jagged and slippery. Miguel produced a rope from a corner of the cave where it had been left in readiness, and bade us make a chain, walking in single file clutching the rope. He showed off a bit, which was a cheering sight, and I saw that Jimmie, too, smiled. Eventually we came to a precipitous dip, where further steps had been hewn in the path. The stream here splashed over the underground rocks in a waterfall which drenched us with its spray. At the foot of these steps a boat was moored. The tunnel spread wide, and now the stream covered the whole ground. Miguel warned us that it was too deep to wade through. We got into the boat, and splashed along for a few yards until we came to a circular chamber of the tunnel, over which Jimmie flashed his torch. Its walls were fluted fanwise like the surface of a shell. Here the river ended in a large pool which swirled in a constant eddy. We landed on a mooring stage at the far shore and from there climbed steadily to the light and air of the exit at the North Arm. It was a boulder-strewn landscape which, if one half-closed one's eyes, resembled a battle-field newly deserted.

On our return late that afternoon Tom Wells said,
'Been through all the caves?'
Jimmie said, 'Yes, but they lack.'
'Lack what?'
'Robinson,' said Jimmie.
'Naturally,' said Wells.

Chapter 9

I was on the patio, pulling faces, when I noticed Tom Wells standing in the shadow of the fountain. I do not know how long he had been standing there, watching me.

The object of my facial contortions was to attempt to discover what it felt like to be Jimmie and Tom Wells respectively. My method was not infallible, but it sometimes served as an aid to perception. I had practised it since childhood. You simply twist your face into the expression of the person whose state of mind and heart you wish to know, and then wait to see what sort of emotions you feel. I had begun with Jimmie. First I considered myself to be standing high and lean, very fair, with a straight wide mouth; and I pulled my mouth straight and wide, I made my eyes close down at the far corners, widening at the inner corners; I raised my eyebrows and furrowed my brow; I put my tongue inside my lower lip, pulled my chin long; my nose, so concentratedly did I imagine it, curving up slightly at the bridge. Then I was self-consciously Jimmie. I said 'Is so', and nodded my head sagely. A sense of helplessness came over me, and I said to myself, though not aloud, 'I lose my nerves.' I placed Robinson in the picture and was filled with awe and exasperation by his standing before me, righteous, austere, a living rebuke. I clasped the fingers of my right hand round an invisible knife, but I did not stab. I was overwhelmed with cousinly love. Widening the inner corner of my eyes, and moving my straight lips soundlessly, I said, 'Is the motor-scooter business', and Robinson replied, 'I have no need of motor-scooters on the island.' But still Jimmie did not stab him, and, as I resumed my normal face, I did not see how he could, in fact, have done so.

I do not know how much of this pantomime was observed by Tom Wells, concealed in the shadow of the fountain, for I had not seen him yet.

Next, I was Tom Wells. I placed my legs solidly apart and sat staring ahead with my bag of lucky charms on my lap, some of them spread out on the patio by my side. I opened my mouth and let the lower lip droop. I turned down the corners of my mouth, and pressed my chin down to make other chins, as flabby as I could think them to be. My skin was mottled and scored with red veins. I rounded my eyes, made them small and light blue, rather watery, and felt beneath them the drag of sallow pouches. My hair was crinkly, partly grey. Moving my lower lip freely I formed the words, 'We're lucky to be alive. A very natural type of woman is my wife.' I had a profound sensation of heat, of sweating about the neck, and my hands were podgy and damp. A longing came over me for the region of Piccadilly Circus and Soho on a summer afternoon; Dean Street, Frith Street, with the dust and paper on the pavement, the smell of garlic and then people scuttling shiftily from door to door, plump men on business, small men popping out of shops in their grey suits and rimless glasses. I longed to be there. But in the middle of this longing I thought, 'No, this isn't Tom Wells. I'm doing Curly Lonsdale.'

And so I started again, the round pouchy eyes, the chin. This time I smiled Tom Wells's smile, which was unlike Curly's, and which showed his upper gums. This made all the difference, and I felt myself raging against the inconvenience of the plane crash, still showing the gums in the smile, and suffering a sensation of furious impatience at the waste of time, the loss of money, and the doubtful fate of my magazine *Your Future*. The more I felt this anger, the more I smiled. When Robinson appeared before me and said 'How are you feeling today?' I clutched my ribs and said, 'Pretty bad. But we're lucky to be alive,' meanwhile closing my fingers round Ethel of the Well, and wishing upon her, 'Bring me luck, Ethel. Don't let Henry marry my wife. Make the Airline company pay compensation. Make the insurance pay up. Make Robinson pay up.' Ethel of the Well changed into a knife. Robinson had stolen my lucky charms. He had done away with my luck. I kept on smiling. 'Where's Ethel, what have you done to Ethel?' I mouthed. Robinson replied, 'They are bad for Miguel. They are evil.' I desired to murder Robinson but I couldn't bring Tom Wells to do that to a goose that might yet lay eggs of gold. Instead I said contemptuously, 'Talking of evil, how's your boy-friend?' Robinson looked at me wearily and walked away. I was still smiling after him with the loose moist lower lip curling like a cup and the wet artificial gums glistening above the top teeth, when I noticed Tom Wells himself in the shadow of the fountain, watching me with his smile. When he saw that he had been observed he nodded, as if to say, 'I can see you.' He walked across to me and said, 'Feeling all right?' I had not pulled my face straight immediately, hoping to mislead him into thinking there was some obvious physical cause for my facial contortions. Instead, I screwed up my eyes and wrinkled my nose, finally passing my hand in an exaggerated gesture across my eyes. I said, 'The sun's horribly strong. I have a headache.' I screwed up my face again so that there should be no mistake.

He stopped smiling and looked at me closely.

'Things worrying you, honey?'

'Oh, just the sun. It gives me a headache.'

I was actually sitting in the shadow of the house and the sun was shining on the opposite half of the patio. Still, it gave off a plausible glare.

'Silly to sit out of doors if the sun gives you a headache,' said Wells.

'Oh, I like the fresh air.'

'Where's your boy-friend?' he said.

'Who?'

'Pardon me,' he said, 'I should have said, Robinson's boy-friend.'

I did not reply.

'Maybe,' he said, 'boy-friend isn't the word after all. *Boy's* the word. But hardly *friend*. Do you get me?'

'I did get your meaning,' I said, 'the first time.'

'Oh, you did?' he said.

I said, 'If you have any complaint against Jimmie, you must make it to him.'

He said, 'Faithful for ever. Well, you've no competition now, have you?'

I went indoors. It was a question whether I was under suspicion and by whom, for the murder of Robinson. I kept thinking of Jimmie's remark, 'You are strong.' Could it reasonably be held that I could have stabbed Robinson, and alone dragged him all the way from the mustard field to the Furnace? The question disturbed me profoundly for two main reasons. One, that my physical ability being proved, I might, when our existence on the island was discovered and the murder disclosed, be under equal suspicion as a killer with Tom Wells and Jimmie. Motives would be probed: what were Mrs Marlow's relations with the dead man? Friendly, unfriendly? I thought of other unanswerable questions that might be asked. I reflected, also, that if Jimmie truly thought it possible that I had killed Robinson, he himself was obviously innocent. The same applied to Tom Wells.

I went into Robinson's study and stood by his tidy desk. I lifted a corner of the desk. It was heavy. Still holding the end of the desk, tilted about nine inches above the ground,

I looked at Robinson's eight-day clock. I watched four aching minutes pass until my arms and fingers gave out. It was not a bad effort, and my strength was not impaired but for the terrible pain in my arms and hands. I supposed that it was not an improbable idea that I could drag Robinson's body up the mountain. I had heard that some types of murderers have access to superhuman strength in the hour of their kill.

It was the beginning of our eleventh week on the island, two weeks since Robinson's disappearance. I had recovered my senses; the stunned feeling had gone. My moods were like a pendulum. In the mornings I was jumpy with impatience and indignation, longing to be active, to clear up the mystery and know where we stood. Towards evening I would feel desolate and nostalgic, brooding on Robinson.

The blue exercise book which Robinson had given me for my journal was full. I took some loose sheets from the drawer of Robinson's desk, the very drawer in which I had discovered the rosary, and this, too, troubled me. However, I set to write as I had intended.

Journal, Monday 19th July.
Supposing that
1) Robinson was murdered by one man only.
2) And that he was killed by stabbing with the knife, in the mustard field, probably between midnight on the 2nd July and dawn on the 3rd.
3) That the murderer carried him to the Furnace.
4) The evidence of this journey, the track of blood, being impossible to conceal, the murderer decided to confuse the evidence. Various garments and objects were soaked in Robinson's blood and scattered indiscriminately along the route.

I note that
5) All the blood-soaked garments we found were either the possessions of Jimmie, myself, or Robinson, or had been

lent to Jimmie and me by Robinson. Nothing was found belonging to Tom Wells or Miguel.

6) The murderer must be one physically capable of carrying or dragging Robinson's body over the mountain to the Furnace.

7) Therefore Miguel is not questionable, although an official investigator may have to rule out the possibility of his being an accomplice.

8) From my point of view, the suspects are Jimmie Waterford and Tom Wells. One is innocent, the other guilty.

9) *Motives*. Jimmie Waterford inherits Robinson's fortune. The disposition of the fortune was under discussion at the time of Robinson's death. The discussions were proving unfavourable to Jimmie.

10) I may remark that he is Robinson's cousin, was brought up by Robinson's mother, and was emotionally attached to Robinson.

11) Also I observe that my friendship with Jimmie did not please Robinson, and one may suppose some discussion on this subject had taken place.

12) Further, I note that Jimmie himself told me the facts of his inheritance. One may think this was strange, if he meditated murder for gain.

13) Tom Wells had a grievance against Robinson for taking away his lucky charms. He discovered the loss of his bag on the night of 2nd July, during which Robinson disappeared.

14) Wells was of the belief, or said he was of the belief, that a homosexual relationship existed between Jimmie and Robinson.

15) As he conveyed this sentiment to me, he also expressed personal horror.

16) I observe that Tom Wells, whether sincerely or not, ascribes the cause of Robinson's death to a supernatural agency.

17) And that Tom Wells exaggerates his injury. He runs about playing the fool with Miguel in the hot sun, but when

there is any useful exertion demanded of him he clasps his ribs as if in pain.

Other Observations :

18) Jimmie Waterford's relations with Robinson, though they were unsatisfactory, were not acrimonious.

19) Tom Wells's mind is opaque. One cannot tell the extent of his superstitions, whether they could so obsess him as to provoke murder, whether the removal of his samples by Robinson was sufficient cause. Of course, one side of his personality is simply materialistic, the other side extremely problematic. (Can he be mad? Can he have murdered unawares?)

20) *Further considerations.* The innocent man will necessarily speculate on the identity of the murderer. His suspicions may fall on the other man. However, he will not be able to rule out the possibility that I am the murderer.

21) It may be expected that the innocent party will avoid as far as possible the company of the likely suspects, e.g. if Jimmie is innocent he will not wish to associate very closely with Wells and me. He may fear us. Wells, if he is innocent, should also react accordingly.

22) The murderer, on the other hand, may wish to maintain a friendly position with his companions, he will be eager to do so, for security's sake.

23) Is it possible to infer guilt or innocence from such attitudes? If Jimmie does not try to avoid Wells and me as if we were potentially dangerous and murderous, does it follow that he is guilty?

24) There remains the question, whether Robinson was killed single-handed.

25) Jimmie is making a memorial to Robinson, consisting of a plain wooden cross on a stand.

I put down the pencil and wished I were at home in Chelsea where once, in the middle of the night, hearing voices and footsteps in the small paved back garden, simply by lifting the telephone I caused policemen to spring up all over the premises as from the dragon's teeth. The police were instantly at the front door and over the garden wall. They marched through the hall and crowded through the kitchen to the back door. Just when they had got the man, another consignment braked up outside, while round the corner of the street four more came walking two abreast at their steady, doom-like and almost contemplative pace. It is true that a dangerous armed lunatic was at this time at large in the district. My intruder turned out to be only the lover of my upstairs lodger making his getaway before dawn. But I appreciated the attention of the Force, as I told it many times as it streamed out of the house, dark blue and corporate, into its line of cars beneath the lamplight.

Telling Agnes about the incident because there was so little to talk to Agnes about, I yet felt wearily sure Ian Brodie would have something to say about it. He said, next day on the telephone, 'You must give that whore a week's notice. A woman in your position can easily let herself in for –'

'How about minding your own business?'

For in any case, even if I had very much wanted to, I would not have had the courage to make a fuss with the girl on such an issue; a woman in my position can easily let herself in for ridicule, can easily be marked down for a wishful widow, and the awful thing about those sort of insinuations, you never know, they might be true.

'Well, if you *want* to keep a disorderly house . . . .' Ian said, his voice rising an octave on the word 'want'.

What struck me as I sat at Robinson's desk with my murder-dossier in front of me was wonder at how I had ever found any resemblance between squeaky Ian Brodie and solemn Robinson.

On the walls were two engravings by Blake, an El Greco reproduction, and a remarkable picture, by or in the manner of Stubbs, of a splendid chestnut horse surrounded by rather wooden people. The question kept tapping at the door, how to reconcile Robinson's tastes, what had been his *centre*? And yet since people do have inconsistencies of taste, or merely inherit the objects they have around them, this question had only symbolic importance. I was thinking of the mystery of his death; all the time I snooped around his rooms I tried to locate his destiny; what indication had he carried about within him, that he should die by murder, at whose hands?

I wandered round the room, looking at Robinson's books behind their glass, and recalling my first repulsion to the neat sets carefully arranged, at this moment I could not see why they had affected me in this way. The bookcases were graceful and the glass fronts enhanced their dignity. And I could think of numerous respectable people who kept their books behind glass. The books themselves seemed admirable, quite enviable; thirty-eight volumes of Bohn's Antiquarian Library, twelve volumes of Bohn's Historical Library, a run of Johnson's *Lives of the Poets*, a number of Pickering reprints, a complete set of the works of Hegel in German alongside some handsome impressive philosophers – Bosanquet, and some whose names I now learned for the first time, Green, Caird, Wallace. The major English and German poets, nothing minor, but possibly Robinson did not care for poetry. There were also numerous publications of the Bacon Society, and I thought, why not? Shakespeare isn't a religion. Some bound monographs of the *Aristotelian Society*, the complete *Golden Bough*. All the Greek dramatists and the Greek and Roman philosophers in the Loeb Classics, Lamennais, Von Hügel, Lacordaire, hundreds of others, and in a case by themselves, the uncut first editions.

When I had first seen the books I had felt sickly, had thought: *whole* sets of *everything*. Big names everywhere. But now, after all, it was a reference library, suitable for an island.

I opened a bookcase by the window wall, where the light was poor, and peering close I found the top shelves filled with mystical theology, about a hundred books – writings of the Christian mystics, concordances and commentaries. The lower shelves were occupied by patristic literature in Latin and Greek, and all the English volumes of the Library of the Fathers. Placed to the left of these, a corner bookcase was devoted to the Marian section, all heavily thumbed and annotated. I thought, well, poor Robinson did at least give thought to the question, Ian Brodie only gives his screeching disapproval supported by misapplied theological quotations.

'Should you desire to possess some of the volumes around us, please to make a choice.' This was Jimmie, standing in the door of Robinson's study. 'Please to retain those which you fancy.'

'Oh, I wouldn't take Robinson's books,' I said.

'Is not now the property of Robinson,' he said mournfully. 'Is mine.'

Jimmie would not avoid me, and so prove his innocence. It was like a game, I played the pipe and he would not dance. I went out of my way to be by his side, watching surreptitiously to see if he flinched from contact with me. He seemed only relieved by this apparent melting on my part. Clearly, I argued with myself, he did not suspect me of murdering Robinson, and his remark, 'You are strong,' had been, most likely, intended to check my intrusive suspicions of himself, as who, whether innocent or not, should say, 'Be careful. If you blame me, I can equally blame you.'

At times I asked myself, what purpose is served by the worry? what was Robinson to you? why bother? It was, I thought, always desirable that justice should be done, but I had never thought of myself as an avenger, a hunterdown of evil. It was one thing to applaud justice, another to bring it about. My fervour surprised me, of course. One thing I do know: I was just as anxious to prevent injustice as to cause justice. There, I was personally endangered, and I could not help feeling that so, to a greater extent, was Jimmie. In fact, without evidence, I suspected Tom Wells of the murder.

And because Jimmie would not treat me as a candidate for the crime, rather than put this down to his guilt I concluded that he, too, had fixed on Tom Wells as the criminal.

It had come as a new idea to me that the island now belonged to Jimmie. Soon afterwards, when Tom Wells and Miguel were out of the way, I said to him,

'We ought to discuss the murder.'

'Is not to be endured. I lose my nerves.'

'If the island is yours, you are responsible for what happens. You must call a conference.'

'Wherefore a conference? Is enough that I grieve in my heart.'

I had not intended confiding in Jimmie, but his answer annoyed me, it struck me as irresponsible.

I said, 'Tom Wells is a killer.'

Jimmie said, 'As for my part, I do not accuse.'

I stood by the open door, actually ready to run for it in case of trouble, since really I knew very little of Jimmie, and said, 'If it wasn't him it must have been you, Jimmie.'

'Not so,' he said.

'In that case,' I said, 'you believe me to be the murderer.'

'Please not to utter such a declaration.'

'Look here,' I said, 'you don't suppose Miguel –'

'Is not within reason. I do not study to accuse.'

'Then perhaps you share the view,' I said, 'with Wells that Robinson was stabbed by a spook?'

'Is folly,' he said, 'to imagine such an irrational occurrence.'

'What *is* your opinion?'

'Opinion? Alas, is not a time for opinions. I sorrow, I lose my nerves.'

After that I reluctantly and tentatively placed Jimmie again under suspicion.

Less than three weeks remained before the pomegranate boat was due. Miguel was off his food. When we managed, by coaxing, to get him to eat something he frequently vomited half an hour later. Sometimes he lay in a fever which lasted about two hours. We dosed and injected him, but his sickness kept recurring. We put it down to 'the terrible strain', without ever mentioning of what. In between his sick attacks he lolled about the patio with Tom Wells, or followed me about the house. He did not seem to take to Jimmie. Not that he took against him, it was only that he seemed to regard Jimmie as a fool, not worth considering.

I often wondered how he worked out Robinson's death in his mind, and whether the question of its cause and agency had occurred to him at all. He was not apparently afraid of us, but had acquired a general nerviness.

I found it hard to believe that Robinson had made no provision for Miguel in the event of his death. I said to Jimmie, 'Robinson must have left a will. Perhaps it is among his papers. Perhaps the island is not yours, after all.'

'Is mine, as I have knowledge, seeing that I already discover the will of Robinson among his papers.'

'Well, you might have mentioned it before.'

'Is our family business.'

'Ah, well, so is the murder, I suppose.'

'Is so, mayhaps.'

'What is to happen to Miguel?'

'Is our family business. I take him to the aunties.'

On Thursday, the twenty-second of July, a plane flew fairly high over the island. There was a drizzle that day. I was in

Robinson's study at the time making a rosary for Miguel out of a string of amber beads that had been amongst the salvage. I had become quite callous about the salvage, and had already made free of the frocks.

Miguel's temperature was normal that day, though he was still sickly and restless. He had been wandering about the house, watching Tom Wells at his writing and me at my rosary-making, and he had drifted silently down to the mustard field where Jimmie had already erected his memorial to Robinson and was now carving some words on the base. About half-past two in the afternoon Miguel came bursting into the house.

'There's an aeroplane coming over from the sky.'

Outside I could see the mist was partially covering the island from the west. The plane approached from the north-east. Jimmie had hurried in from the mustard field and made for the gun-room where the rockets were kept. I fetched the big red signal kite from Robinson's study and brought it out to the patio where I found Tom Wells gazing skyward and clutching his ribs. The plane was over the island and away before Jimmie came back to demand the key of the gun-room which I kept on a string round my neck.

I handed him the kite. 'Unwind it,' I said. 'I'll fetch the rockets.'

'Too late,' said Tom Wells, 'the plane's gone.'

'It may come back.'

There was insufficient breeze to carry the kite but we fired rockets at intervals throughout the afternoon and the following night. There was no further sign of the plane, which must have observed nothing special to report about our island, a minute green rock in the Atlantic. But the excitement of our rockets far into the night had a good effect on Miguel. Although he had a fever next morning, he was in better spirits and by the afternoon he was recovered. As there was a high breeze that day, I gave him Robinson's splendid red kite with its long sequin tail which previously had been forbidden to him. I showed him how to fly it, and as he stood unwinding, holding the heavy apparatus with difficulty, he said,

'Is it mine to keep?'

'See if you can signal the aeroplane to come back,' I said.

'Is it mine to keep?'

'You'll have to ask Jimmie,' I said.

'Does it belong to Jimmie now that Robinson's dead?' he said, quite casually, with his eye on the kite.

'Yes. The island belongs to Jimmie.'

I could see that he was beginning to forget his loss of Robinson, less than three weeks after his death, and I was thankful, because his brooding had been a worry; and I wondered if Brian, though older and different, might by now have accepted my death.

The pomegranate boat was expected between the eighth and tenth of August. I allowed myself to sit gazing out to sea in the hope that it would appear before time, and also in dread, since the boat would find us with a murder on our hands. Meanwhile I made the rosary for Miguel. It was a difficult process, for the tiny holes in the golden beads were too small for the needle; and as I had to make each hole larger with a canvas-bodkin, I worked slowly. I had not quite finished it when Jimmie announced the completion of the memorial. Miguel and I went down to the mustard field. The memorial had been placed at the spot where Robinson's blood-stained jacket and the clasp-knife had been found. It consisted of a wooden cross, very neatly made and joined, although the left arm was longer than the right, and the shaft was set at a slight angle. On the plain block base was inscribed in uneven lettering:

This filled up the whole of the space on the front of the block. 'Is no further room for R.I.P.' said Jimmie. 'Initially I did aim to insert R.I.P. but is not possible. The first letters I create too tall, and then, behold, is no more space.'

Miguel said to Jimmie, pointing at the memorial, 'Is that Robinson?'

'How is that you mean?' said Jimmie.

Miguel looked baffled at this question and though Jimmie pressed him he would not answer. I supposed he thought of the memorial as a sort of statue of Robinson when, later on in the house, he asked me, 'Why is one of Robinson's arms longer than the other?' and after considering his meaning I said, 'Oh, you mean the memorial?' And sometimes, though he referred to it as a memorial, he seemed to hold some sort of pathetic fallacy: 'Won't the memorial be cold out there all night?' He seemed to feel that Robinson's real presence had been transformed into the memorial. It was always impossible to know exactly what was going on in his mind.

The more I pondered the murder the more did I come to think of Robinson as a kind of legendary figure since it was hard to believe that only a few weeks had passed since he had led me on my first visit to the Furnace. Perhaps, even at that time, he had assumed near-mythical dimensions in my eyes. I saw him now as an austere sea-bound hero, a noble heretic, who to follow his mystical destiny, had hidden himself away from the world with only a child-disciple for company. I supposed he had recognized in Miguel a strong unformed religious potentiality. Robinson himself was essentially a religious man. Jimmie had once, in the manner of one who had a relative bitten with an eccentric ambition, referred to Robinson's desire for spiritual advancement. In thinking of Robinson, I had to perform an act of imaginative distortion in that I could not think of him as a part of the present tense, a human creature who had been born into a particular age and at a particular point of developed doctrine – I vaguely thought of him as having no proper station in life like the rest of us. I thought of his rescue work at the time of the crash, his nursing us to health, the burial of the dead, and his patience with our ungrateful intrusion into his elected solitude. That he should have met his end at the hands of one of his beneficiaries seemed to me the essence of his tragedy. And in this interesting light he took on the heroic character of a pagan pre-Christian victim of expiation.

I used to spend a lot of time in Robinson's rooms, recalling his attempts to entertain us with his Rossini recordings, and sometimes imparting information about the history and legends of the island. Robinson's evenings had clearly been an effort to him; I recalled the prevalent feeling of his trying to bring order out of chaos in a schoolmasterly way, never really trusting the evening to go smoothly unless he organized it for us.

I was surprised at the clarity and number of his incidental remarks, which my memory, like a recording instrument, now played back to me. And for the first time I recalled certain pieces of information which I had not really listened to when Robinson had imparted them.

He had told us that if the island was the southernmost part of Atlantis, as the legends suggested, this would extend the current speculations about the size of Atlantis by fifteen hundred miles. The island had been a peninsula, famous for its pomegranate orchards which had been planted by King Arthur. Another legend told of a beautiful northern princess who had been carried there by a half-human demon and imprisoned in the mountain beneath the Furnace. From there her screams attracted a shepherd who gallantly threw himself in the Furnace to be imprisoned with her. The scream could still be heard whenever the crater was disturbed by an object entering it. The lovers can only be released if a priest is prepared to bless them and die immediately afterwards. Another group of legends claimed the island to be the home of the Greek Hesperus, and assigned an oracular function to the Furnace.

Chance fragments of Robinson's conversation recurred to me at this time, although when he told these stories I had usually been thinking of something else, had been occupied with Jimmie's intriguing qualities, or burned-up with irritation at Tom Wells, or day-dreaming about Chelsea. In fact, it was not until some months after I had left the island, when I was questioned about its history, that I remembered points in Robinson's conversations that I had previously forgotten. And even now I keep remembering new facts which Robinson gave us then, night after night, as if compelled to do so lest we should run amok.

When I sat in Robinson's rooms summoning up his presence, it was not only the substance of his conversation that returned to me, but also the tone of his voice, even, rhythmical, almost a chant, which had a slightly mesmeric effect:

'The history is obscure. . . .

'Traditional hermits' home. Five of them . . .one on each Arm, one on each Leg, and one . . .

'A few Arabs, Danes . . .

'A line of Portuguese have successively owned the island.

'Yes, eccentrics, I dare say . . .

'The history is obscure. . . .

'The island has always been privately owned.

'Bought and sold. . . .

'Smugglers' hide-out, of course. . . .

'Too small to need more than nominal protection. . . .

'Ruling powers not really interested. . . .

'The history is obscure. . . .

'Most of the craters active six hundred years ago. . . .

'Vasco da Gama's fleet nosed in. . . .'

In the late afternoon of the day when Jimmie finished the memorial I mooned round Robinson's rooms, flicking a duster, touching books, and almost hearing his voice intone on the subject of the island. On a side table lay his reading glasses face-down with the shafts upright, in the position in which he had left them. From curiosity, and because I had been considering the peculiar essence of Robinson, I tried on the glasses. Usually when, for some idle reason, I have tried on other people's glasses everything has looked out of focus, has appeared to swim, as if I were unwell. I expected some mild sensation of this kind when I tried on Robinson's glasses, but I did not expect what happened. The room swung over and round in a swivel movement. The books leaped from the shelves and piled over the carpet. Everything on the tables and the desk whirled on to the floor, and even then did not stay still. I myself staggered and reeled with the room, and as I clung to the back of a heavy leather chair the El Greco *Agony* flew off the wall, to which it had been very tightly clamped, just missing me. As for Robinson's glasses, they had not been on my nose for the space of a blink, but I did not need their absence to tell me that the room was rocking in any case, without their aid. The pitch and toss grew gradually milder. I fixed my eye on one of the books spread open on the floor. It steadied up, so that I could see the bookplate on the inside of the cover, and it remained quite still, '*Nunquam minus solus quam cum solus*'. I caught sight of Miguel running past the window with a grin on his face. He came inside and opened the study door, smiling excitedly.

'Mr Tom is under his bed,' he said.

'Do you often have earthquakes here?'

'I think so. Jimmie has cut his hand on a piece of glass.'

'Are they all as severe as this?' I said.

'All what?'

'Severe. Bad. Are they all bad, like this?'

'They aren't bad. Robinson said so.'

'I call it bad,' I said.

'Mr Tom is under his bed.'

Tom Wells must have emerged from his shelter, for he was now crossing the patio looking pale, flabby and troubled in the half-light.

'Where's your boy-friend?' he said sharply to me.

Jimmie emerged from the kitchen door with his hand bound in a towel like a huge stump.

'I have received a shock,' he said.

'Look here, Waterford,' said Tom Wells, 'you own this island, don't you?'

'Is mine,' said Jimmie, unwinding the towel slightly, then quickly, at the sight of his blood, replacing the fold.

'Take it from me,' said Wells, 'you're going to have to pay me damages.'

'Alas, where have you been damaged?' said Jimmie, nursing the towel.

'I'm covered with knocks. I'm going to claim damages.'

'Tell him it's an Act of God,' I said to Jimmie.

'Is an act from God,' said Jimmie.

'Like the murder,' said Wells.

'How do you mean?' said Jimmie. But Tom Wells walked tremulously into the house.

Miguel had started clearing up the mess, as if by routine. I joined him in the kitchen, separating the broken crockery and glass from that which was left intact, or merely cracked. Very soon, however, the delayed effects of the earthquake overtook me, and the lamplit kitchen went out of focus, swimming before my eyes as if I had tried on someone else's glasses. I went to my room and lay down, not sure if, on entering the room, I had encountered Tom Wells again, startled and guilty, outside the door of my room, or if I had imagined it.

Next day Jimmie had to set up the memorial again. It had toppled over during the earthquake. Miguel, however, did not accompany him, but instead hung round me to see the completion of the rosary which was now quite presentable. I fixed to the chaplet a cross which I had made, with difficulty, from the smallest of the amber beads threaded with thin wire. Miguel was magnetized by this new trinket, and when I showed him how to use it he was not content until he had mastered the technique, holding between his frail brown fingers and thumb glittering bead by bead, nodding his head in time to the repetitive prayers, completely under the spell. It crossed my mind how easily he was influenced. '*Santa Maria*,' he said suddenly. '*Mãe de Deus*,' and I realized he had heard the rosary recited in his infancy.

By way of conversation, and because he liked to know the ins and outs of anything, once it had captured his interest, I said, 'It ought to be blessed by a priest, but as there isn't a priest on the island I dare say you can gain all the indulgences without a blessing.' These words, which he but dimly understood, dazzled him considerably. I suppose the unknown element, 'indulgences', to be gained from a 'priest's blessing', gave extra glamour to his rosary. He questioned me all afternoon.

'What is indulgences?' 'Can you pray on Ethel of the Well?' 'Is Mr Tom a Catholic?' 'Is Jimmie . . . ?'

He displayed the rosary to Tom Wells at the first opportunity.

Wells said: 'That's an R.C. item. Robinson wouldn't have approved.'

Miguel sensed danger and hurried off with his treasure.

'You should respect Robinson's wishes,' said Wells. 'He always said how easily anyone could corrupt the boy.'

'You speak too late,' I said, 'since I've already started to corrupt him.'

'It isn't a laughing matter.'

'Very true.'

Something else about his words sounded odd to me: I could hardly believe that Robinson's murderer would say, 'You should respect Robinson's wishes.'

Chapter 10

IT IS not that I judge people by their appearance, but it is true that I am fascinated by their faces. I do not stare in their presence. I like to take the impression of a face home with me, there to stare at and chew over it in privacy, as a wild beast prefers to devour its prey in concealment.

As a means of judging character it is a misleading practice and as for physiognomy the science, I know nothing of that. The misleading element, in fact, provides the essence of my satisfaction. In the course of deciphering a face, its shape, tones, lines and droops as if these were words and sentences of a message from the interior, I fix upon it a character which, though I know it to be distorted, never quite untrue, never entirely true, interests me. I am as near the mark as myth is to history, the apocrypha to the canon. I seek no justification for this habit, it is one of the things I do. Most of all, I love to compare faces. I have seen a bus conductor who resembles a woman don of my acquaintance, I have seen the face of Agnes throwing itself from side to side in the pulpit; I make a meal of these.

All the time I was on the island I set considerable store by faces; and in the absence of normal criteria of judgement, I fell back on intuitions of faces whenever I was frightened.

The facial resemblance between Tom Wells and Curly Lonsdale lay more in the expression than the actual features. Curly's mouth was not so loose. But both had the habit of keeping their mouths open all the time, and you would sometimes think they were smiling when they were not.

Curly Lonsdale once remarked, 'Life is based on blackmail', but I have since come to think he had himself in mind, not as the blackmailer but the blackmailed. I think he had in mind the fact that he had always operated within an inch of the law; and 'life' for Curly consisted of those standards of behaviour which he had set up for himself.

The pomegranate boat was expected in nine or ten days. I was more and more impatient, and at the same time apprehensive. It gave rise to a feeling not unlike guilt to imagine in advance the men spilling ashore on the white beach. 'Where's Robinson?' Or perhaps they spoke only Portuguese, and would question Jimmie or Miguel. Tom Wells and I would look on, as if we were both of a piece. And they would, in turn, look at us, would of course put us under arrest. Probably weeks and months of detention and inquiries would transpire before I could go home.

Tom Wells found me alone in Robinson's study and said, 'There's something I want to say to you privately.'

I said, 'If it's blackmail, sorry I'm not rich.'

He said, 'I don't understand.'

'True enough,' I said. 'No one will believe you if you try to pin the murder on me.'

'Honey, I wouldn't dream of framing you. What I wanted to say was –'

'Why are you blackmailing Jimmie?' I thought for a moment that he was still smiling, but I was wrong, it was his loose mouth. He said, 'If you know what's good for you, you'll keep your mouth shut.'

'I do not, as a rule, go about with it hanging open.'

'That's the bitch,' he said. 'You were always a bitch to Robinson.'

'You are trying to blackmail Jimmie.'

'I'm negotiating for a settlement. I've sustained damages on his island. If he doesn't want a reckon-up with me, he'll get it elsewhere.'

'You'll never get away with that,' I said.

'Listen,' he said, 'be reasonable. Do you want to put

your boy-friend in the way of difficulties?'

I said, 'What difficulties?' and looked out of the window to see if Jimmie or Miguel were about.

'What I want to say to you,' he said, 'is this. We'd better have an understanding about the murder.'

'In my opinion,' I said, 'it was occasioned by a supernatural force.'

He looked at me to see what I meant, and was not sure. He said, 'That's a good enough yarn for ourselves, dear – or rather, *was* until your boy-friend settled down a bit. He must have been worried, naturally, after what he did. But you mustn't talk about the supernatural to the dicks, dear, it makes them cross as hell.'

'No,' I said, 'I shall not say things like that.' I looked out of the window.

'Now you're talking sense, sweetie, you're talking good sense. Now, we'd better have an understanding. I did think of suicide. What do you think of suicide?'

'If you care to commit suicide,' I said, 'that's your affair. But I'm bound to point out it is a mortal sin.'

'You playing dumb, dear?'

I said, 'I don't agree to put out the tale that Robinson committed suicide,' and took another look out of the window to see if anyone was nearby.

'Then it'll have to be an accident. Robinson had an accident. He slipped and fell on the mountain and he broke his neck. His face was badly bashed in, d'you see, not recognizable. We buried him among the victims of the crash, poor chap.'

'Anything else?' I said. 'Because I'm busy at the moment.'

'We'll burn the evidence tonight,' he said, 'and we shall sign the statement tomorrow.'

'What statement?'

'The one I'm going to prepare. I just wanted to know

whether you preferred suicide or an accident. Mind you, suicide would be sound, because he was a bit touched in the head, Robinson.'

I said, 'Have you consulted Jimmie?'

'About the damages? That's another matter, you don't come into that. We sign the statement about Robinson's misfortune *after* Jimmie has signed his agreement with me about the damages.'

'Has Jimmie agreed to swear that Robinson was killed in an accident?'

'Oh yes, and he'll come across with it. What d'you take him for?'

'I don't believe you.' There was no sign of anyone from the window. I did not know if Jimmie or Miguel were near the house.

'D'you suppose he's going to give himself up?' said Wells.

'No; why should he?'

Tom Wells said, 'Yes, *why* should he?' He looked at me in a frightening way and said, 'You're not such an unnatural bitch that you'd shop your man, are you?' He laid his large hand on my shoulder, gripping painfully.

I said, 'Take your hand off my shoulder.'

He said, 'You'll sign the statement.'

I said, 'Take your hand off my shoulder or I shall scream.'

He dropped his hand, and said, 'You'll sign the statement.'

I said, 'I don't see why I should put Jimmie's money your way.'

'What you say, honey,' he said, 'is natural enough. I'd give you a slice, but you won't need it, that's honest, if you know how to handle your boy-friend. You're on to a good thing there, and some of it's in motor-scooters, – you can't go wrong with motor-scooters.'

'You have forgotten Miguel,' I said.

He said, 'Tom Wells never forgets.'

'He saw the blood,' I said, 'and the bloodstains and the knife.'

'Naturally,' said Wells, 'he saw the blood and the knife. Anyone can see the youngster's backward. And he has a lot of imagination, and he has a touch of fever besides being a bit peculiar in the head – not surprising when you think of the unnatural life. No one's going to listen to Miguel about the blood and the knife.'

'Anything else? Because I'm busy.'

He said, 'You'll sign the agreement.' Out of the window I saw Jimmie and Miguel walking across the patio. I said to Tom Wells, 'Go to hell,' and left him.

Ten minutes later I saw Miguel sidle up to Tom Wells on the patio. I had long been disabused of the idea that a child is an instinctive judge of character, but I never ceased to wonder at the attraction Miguel felt towards Tom Wells, who moreover treated him quite roughly.

'Sign his paper,' said Jimmie. 'Is best.'

'You must be mad,' I said.

'Is so,' said Jimmie, 'that I want my head examined. But I see is best to sign.'

'You must be guilty,' I said, 'of killing Robinson.'

'Is not so. Never do I think to take care of Robinson.'

'Then I'd see Tom Wells in hell before I would sign his statement. And mind you don't sign any agreement to pay him money.'

'Is a dangerous man,' said Jimmie. 'You do not conceive what story he has prepared, in the event we do not sign.'

'He will accuse you of the murder. Don't worry, the motive of Robinson's inheritance doesn't count for everything. The police usually find the guilty man; and if you're innocent, simply say so.'

'Is not the story which he has prepared,' said Jimmie. 'He has prepared to accuse you, that you have stabbed with the knife.'

'I really don't think that would be believed,' I said. 'I don't think I look strong enough to drag a body up the mountain.'

'Tom Wells has prepared to accuse that you did knife Robinson at the dawn in the mustard field, and he accuses that he has heard you return to the house and confide these doings to me, which this Wells declares he has heard. Whereafter together we depart to the place where is the body of Robinson, and we transport this body to the Furnace.'

I said, 'Why should *I* kill Robinson?'

'Is the declaration of Tom Wells that you have done the crime on purpose to gain for me the fortune. Whereafter you marry me.'

I said, 'You must see now, Jimmie, that Tom Wells is the criminal.'

'I do not accuse. Is dangerous to accuse. Mayhaps in consequence he should request a duel. He is entitled to make such demand. Then is mayhaps blood shed. Is serious to say to a man, "Behold, you have killed." Is better to sign the statement.'

This speech gave me no pleasure.

'Do you really think,' I said, 'anyone would believe his story?'

'Is better to sign,' he said.

I wrote my island journal that night, Saturday, the thirty-first July. I did not know at the time that it was to be the last entry, but I realized for the first time that my journal might be a fateful sort of document, might come in useful, and so I wrote with special thought.

1) I begin by stating that I have reached the conclusion that T. Wells murdered Robinson.

2) I may remark that the motive of gain which might lay suspicion on Jimmie Waterford or on myself is not likely to be thought unquestionably conclusive. The question would arise, might not the transparency of this motive deter a potential murderer? Further, would not the criminal take the utmost care to conceal his guilt? It must be remembered that the bloodstained articles which were found between the mustard field and the Furnace had been in use by Jimmie, Robinson and myself. Nothing belonging to Tom Wells was found. Far from contributing to the case against Jimmie and me, this casts suspicion, I believe, on Tom Wells.

3) Also, I observe that from the type and position of the bloodstained articles they had been deliberately planted there.

4) Tom Wells is a blackmailer. He has put it to me that we all three sign a statement to the effect that Robinson died of an accident. I say 'put it to me' but in fact he seemed to think it certain I would agree. I gained the impression from Wells that he was counting on my affection for Jimmie, and my desire to cover up for him.

The price of this hushing up of the murder is a sum of money to be extorted from Jimmie.

But I have further information from Jimmie about Wells's intentions. Failing our agreement to sign his statement, he proposes to inform the Portuguese authorities that I murdered Robinson by stabbing with a knife, subsequently persuading Jimmie to assist me in disposing of the body; motive being to acquire for Jimmie Robinson's fortune, and later to marry Jimmie.

5) Jimmie tells me he is prepared to sign the statement. This may mean one of four things:
    i) That he is guilty.
    ii) That he is innocent but afraid of being implicated, or desires to avoid trouble in general.
    iii) That he desires to save me from being implicated.

iv) That he is in league with Tom Wells.

6) I favour the proposition that Jimmie is innocent but wants to avoid trouble and so is prepared to acquiesce in Tom Wells's demands.

7) I leave the possibility of Jimmie's guilt to consider the question of Tom Wells.

8) I know him to be a blackmailer in one instance. I think he may be a professional blackmailer.

   If that is so, and Robinson had evidence of it, that would provide a motive for murder.

   I am thinking of the papers which were missing from Tom Wells's bag when it was restored to him by Robinson, and about which Wells made a fuss (see Journal 1st July), and I think it possible that his luck-and-occult racket is a cover for trade in blackmail, and a means to it. I am thinking of all the people who write and tell him their secrets.

9) It is possible that the body may be retrieved from the Furnace.

10) I do not think of signing Tom Wells's statement.

I had been using loose sheets of paper for my journal since I had filled the blue exercise book which Robinson had given to me. I slipped the sheets inside the back cover of the exercise book and put it in a drawer in my room where I kept it.

The question of signing the statement was giving me more trouble than I had allowed to appear in the journal. The morals of the question apart, I felt strongly that it would be the greatest folly to falsify evidence in a way that might easily be detected by expert criminologists, and I also had a horror of placing myself in Tom Wells's power.

I felt that in opposing Jimmie and Wells I was up against two different types of the melodramatic mind; one coloured by romance, the other by crime. We were on the same island but in different worlds.

Although these things were clear to me, I was afraid of pressure. I feared the united pressure of Jimmie and Tom Wells, and, more, the pressure of the scheme's expedient attractions. If successful, it would facilitate my homegoing – no interrogations, no unpleasantness in the newspapers. I was beginning to think up an idea that really there was no reason why the scheme should not be successful, when I decided to put the temptation out of my reach. I went to find Miguel. He was fishing in the lake. 'Miguel,' I said, 'do you know what a lie is?'

He said, 'Yes.'

'What is a lie?'

He screwed up his face to search his memory, then he said, 'When you say something is different from what you think it is.' It sounded like a set piece of Robinson's teaching. Although Miguel was truthful, I was not sure that he understood the formula.

'Do you remember,' I said, 'the day that Robinson disappeared?'

He screwed up his face as if to recall something and I understood that he was trying to remember the date.

'I mean, do you remember what happened on that day, and what we did?'

'Yes, Mr Tom found the knife and Robinson's jacket. We went to look for Robinson.'

I said, 'What do you think happened to Robinson?'

'Someone killed him,' he said.

'Who do you think killed him?'

'The Parroveevil,' he said.

'Say it again.'

He repeated it twice, and presently I discerned the influence of Tom Wells and his Power of Evil.

'Suppose someone said that Robinson fell down, alone by himself on the mountain, and was killed?'

'Who said it?'

'*Suppose* someone said it, what would that be?'

He said, 'A mistake.'

I said, 'Do you remember the things we found when we were looking for Robinson?'

He said, 'All the clothes.'

'That's right. What did they look like?'

'They were all over blood,' he said.

'Suppose,' I continued, 'that one of us said we didn't find any clothes at all, and that there wasn't any blood?'

'That would be silly,' he said.

'Would it be true?'

'No, they must be making a mistake.'

I thought, what odds if he doesn't know what a lie is, so long as he speaks the truth? And by his puzzled look I was satisfied that the present conversation would stick in his mind. It would be difficult, now, to persuade him that he had dreamt the evidence of Robinson's death.

The swimming suit was slightly too big for me, but it was the best I could find among the salvage. I regretted not availing myself of it earlier, when I had been obliged to sit enviously on the shore of the lake and watch Jimmie and Robinson splashing about in bathing trunks and Miguel swimming naked, diving like a rocket. There had been no garment for me to bathe in. 'Bathe in nothing at all,' Jimmie had advised, 'and we avert our gaze.'

'There's a woman's swimming suit amongst the salvage,' Robinson had said.

I had come to the lake to cool off after a violent encounter with Tom Wells and Jimmie. I had told them both at breakfast that I would not sign the statement, and I deliberately spoke in front of Miguel, hoping that he would take in something of the meaning rather than the mere vibrations.

'Better to sign,' said Jimmie.

146

'Look, let's all get together and discuss it in private,' said Wells, looking at Miguel.

'There's nothing to discuss.'

'We meet at two p.m.,' said Wells. 'That's final.'

'Better to sign,' said Jimmie.

I said to Jimmie, 'You make me sick.'

He sprang up and banged the table. 'Is on your behalf that I make you sick.'

I had not seen Jimmie lose his temper before. I was taken aback and must have shown it, for Tom Wells was quick to follow this advantage with a loud-voiced, 'You'll sign, if it's the last thing you do. Robinson died of an accident – get it?'

Jimmie turned on him and said, 'Get it – is not nice to address a lady like the thunder, get it.'

'Come away, Miguel,' I said loftily. 'Come with me.'

He came hesitantly. Tom Wells called after me. 'Two p.m.'

At two o'clock I was cooling myself in the lake. I had avoided the house all day and had brought food to eat by the lake. I was regretting that I had not availed myself of the salvaged bathing dress in our early days on the island. I would have preferred the sea, but Robinson had warned us of the sharks. Apart from the streams which scored the island, and which were often only ankle-deep, the lake was the only bathing place.

It was wonderfully soothing and the blue-green effect was only slightly diminished when one was actually in the water. I think the colour was caused by some mineral in the lake water rather than reflection from the sky; when I sent a splash into the air, it looked like a shower of transparent blue gems. Making big splashes to some extent alleviated the apprehensive pain about my stomach, a physical pain which I had been going about with for the last two weeks, and which I realized had been nibbling inside me since Robinson's disappearance.

It had been a favourite game of Bluebell, when Robinson was swimming in the lake, to race along the bank trying to catch the glittering blue beads of water which he threw in her direction. I caught sight of the cat on the bank as I dabbled around, saw it was trying to egg me on to play. It did this by planting its forepaws together on the very verge of the lake and waggling its hindquarters ready to spring. The technique of the game, on the swimmer's part, was to send a shower of spray a little above and in front of the cat, and then she would leap, almost fly in the air after the elusive drops. Bluebell did not seem to mind when it occasionally drenched her, but would shake the blue water off her head and crouch for the next spring. I swam in to the edge and obliged her with a high-thrown handful of lake water. She gave a beautiful leap, her slate-blue coat looking far more blue beside the lake. I swam farther round, churning out Bluebell's shower with the back of my hand. 'Come on, Bluebell,' I called to her, 'water's good for the nerves.' I wondered how soon the cat would tire, and decided to see if she would follow me all round the lake, trotting, crouching, leaping, in her wonderful rhythm. We were more than half-way round when she got bored, and browsed off among the ferns towards the cliff edge. I drifted for a small while, then decided to set off again towards the bank where I had left my clothes. I did not intend to return to the house just yet; I had it in mind to walk down the cliff-path and through the copse of blue-gum trees to the Pomegranate beach, there to let the white sand trickle through my toes and fingers. I started cutting across the lake, and when I had almost reached the middle I caught sight of Tom Wells disappearing behind some shrubbery near the spot where I had left my clothes. At first I thought he was lying in wait for me behind the shrubbery, but as I came up to the bank I saw him retreating farther off, shuffling up to the house.

The key of the gun-room, which I usually kept on a string

round my neck, was missing from among my clothes, where I had left it. The pain above my stomach returned.

I dressed quickly and went in search of Jimmie. He was drinking brandy in Robinson's study. When he saw me he said:

'Alas, I am abased to the servile floor.'

I shivered, for in my haste I had not dried myself properly. I said, 'I'd like a drink.'

He poured some brandy for me. 'I lose my nerves.'

I said, 'Wells has stolen the key of the gun-room from me.'

He jumped up. 'He has assaulted you to obtain this key?'

'No, I left it lying about.'

Jimmie filled his glass and said, 'Is my key – lo, all is mine.'

I said, 'Take care what you do. He has probably armed himself.'

'He is angered in the extreme, that you do not sign the statement today,' Jimmie said. 'Thus mayhaps he shall insist by pointing the pistol. Is not humorous.'

'Have you signed his statement?'

'No, no. Is fruitless if all do not agree.'

'Have you signed any agreement to pay him the money?'

'No, is fruitless if all do not agree to Robinson's accident.'

I said, 'I have a sort of weapon against Tom Wells.'

'Yes, yes,' said Jimmie. 'I do recall the pistol.'

'I don't mean the pistol,' I said. 'I mean my journal. It is a sort of evidence, a dossier. People would find it difficult to reconcile Tom Wells's story with the journal.'

Jimmie was only half-listening. 'If you please,' he said, 'is best to place the little gun into my charge. Is necessary, in the event that I am obliged to protect you.'

I kept the baby Browning in the pocket of my coat. I am always rather afraid of firearms; and without actually believing they can go off by themselves, I have one of those shadowy fears that they will. Every morning I had checked

149

the Browning to see if the safety-catch was still on, and sometimes in the night I would get up to have another look; that was the relationship between myself and the automatic.

I said to Jimmie, 'I may need the automatic myself. In fact, I think I need it now more than you do.'

'Is like this,' Jimmie said. 'Is not nice to have a gun except in the event that you understand it. Many ladies do not understand what is a gun. In the event that words should occur, pouff – the lady will shoot and the gentleman is killed.'

'I ought to keep it for security. I don't like the thought of Tom Wells having the key of the gun-room.'

'Is my intention to arrange that he should render up that key.'

'My God!' I said. 'If I give you the pistol there will be another murder.'

'No, no,' said Jimmie. 'Is to go too far. Never in my life do I shoot to kill. I understand what is a gun. Is best for you to give to me my gun, then is no killing in the event that you make mistakes.'

I did not miss the words 'my gun'. The automatic was undoubtedly Jimmie's property, and I felt, if it came to that, he could easily force his gun from me. But I was more impressed by the idea that I might kill Tom Wells, should I be provoked to wield the automatic against him. In fact, I thought, this would be very likely, since I was on edge with fear of him, and the possibility of what he might do in the days ahead. Seven or eight days, I thought, is a long time when you can kill a man in less than a second, and so complicate your life. Self-defence is all very well, but two murders on the island . . .

'Is best,' said Jimmie, 'not to have a gun if you are not experienced with shooting. In the course of the hostilities I have had the occasion . . .'

Like a fool, I went and fetched the Browning. Even as I handed it over I regretted it; I was insecure, and overcome with a feeling of distrust for Jimmie.

I left him immediately, resolved to make a record in my journal of my having given him the gun, and the reasons why I had done so.

The journal was gone from its drawer. It was nowhere in my room. I had been altogether counting on it to counteract Tom Wells's accusation against me. Of course, it contained no direct proof, but it had struck me, on reading it through, that it was not at all the sort of journal that anyone would write who was gradually meditating murder. And also it contained the 'dossier' of the murder itself, the notes of my suspicions and reflections which I had intended to hand over to the Portuguese. I set particular store by my theory that Robinson had discovered some blackmailing activity of Wells, and so been silenced.

For some reason, when I was satisfied that the blue exercise book was not in my room, I felt light-headed. I felt carefree and reckless. I went to Robinson's apartments and put a recording of Mozart on the gramophone, poured myself a drink, lit a cigarette, sat back, and closed my eyes. Bluebell, who had sidled into the room with me, leapt on to my lap and, purring loudly, started to pummel me with her paws, prior to nestling down. When the record came to an end I turned it over and had some more Mozart. I had another drink. When I felt I was bored with music, I cast round for a novel and found that Robinson's few novels had apparently been chosen for their bibliographical charms. I pulled out of the case a leather-bound volume of a novel, and opened it in the middle of a chapter. The eighteenth-century typography, with its s's like f's, irritated me. I threw it on to a nearby sofa. I put on another record, poured myself another drink. I took up the book again:

Now the agonies which affected the mind of Sophia rather augmented than impaired her beauty; for her tears added brightnefs to her eyes, and her breafts rofe higher with her fighs. Indeed, no one hath feen beauty in its highest luftre, who hath never feen it in diftrefs. . . .

I put it by, and settled down to the interesting thought of how like I was at this moment to my sister Julia. There is something about too much worry that brings out Julia in me, a temporary reaction which is typical of her constant behaviour. Julia spends her life putting discs on and off her electric gramophone, switching on the television, switching it off, pouring herself a drink, taking up a book, throwing it on a nearby sofa, lifting the telephone, then changing her mind. And I mused on other occasions of special stress when on the other hand, I was Agnes to the life. That was when I had been over-excited by some event, such as a play, or a letter with a surprise cheque, or a party where I had chattered all night very successfully and been much talked to. My hangover, perhaps a kind of protection against excitability, took the form of a fat-headed domestic triviality, and I would make it a big issue to consider how long, to the very month, the curtains had been in use, resolving to clean out cupboards that had not been touched for fifteen years, writing out timetables to follow, writing out my expenditure in one column, my income in another, adding up and glumly comparing them. This would last but a few hours, but Agnes did it all her life.

While I pondered the genetic question involved in these self-observations, the irrelevant idea flashed upon me that Tom Wells was the sort of person likely to hide my journal under his mattress.

I was almost right. The blue exercise book was under the counterpane at the foot of his bed. I examined it and found it intact, loose pages and all. I had ascertained his presence on the patio before entering his room. He had been sitting out there, looking suddenly quite horrible with a hand on each knee, and the key of the gun-room hanging conspicuously round his neck. Now, from his window, I saw the back of his head above the chair where he was seated, and I thought how stupid he was.

It was about five o'clock. I had just time to reach my destination and return before the mists should fall. I quickly cut a square piece out of Robinson's waterproof – the handiest thing I could find for the purpose – and, wrapping my notebook in this to protect it from dampness, I set off for the secret tunnel which led from the cliffs at the Pomegranate Bay to the South Arm. It was my plan to conceal my journal near the South Arm end of the tunnel, so that there should be no chance of Wells coming upon it by accident. He had never been to the caves, and seldom walked far beyond the vicinity of the house. A visit to the scene of the accident had been his longest venture, and he had gone there only to assure himself that his missing papers were not among the debris at the spot where he had been found. He had returned from this visit, complaining of exhaustion and clutching his ribs.

I chose the Pomegranate Bay tunnel because it was sufficiently near at hand to enable me to reach it and return before the fall of the mist, and yet not too near. The tunnel whose entrance led from the cliff just behind the house to the Furnace was, I felt, too nearby to be safe from anyone really on the hunt. And, of course, the cave on the North Arm was too far away, although I would gladly have hidden my book that distance from Tom Wells.

I had only got as far as the beach when I realized I had forgotten to bring a light, without which it was impossible to penetrate the tunnel. I returned as quickly as possible up the mountain path. I stopped only to stuff my package out of sight for the time being in a hollow at the bole of a tree, covering it up with whin, and placing some small black

pebbles on the path in the form of a cross, to mark the place.
I saw that a light mist had begun to curl round the mountain.

There was a powerful flashlamp about nine inches long
in Robinson's study; all the others were weak, the batteries
running out. It usually lay on the wide window ledge.

In Robinson's study I found Tom Wells sitting at the
desk.

'Good evening,' he said. 'So I murdered Robinson to
keep him quiet?'

'You know best,' I said.

'I'm a blackmailer, you say?'

'Yes, that's what I say.'

'Well,' he said, 'naturally you'll be disappointed to hear
that I've destroyed your little notebook.'

'You haven't stolen my journal?' I said, making frightened eyes.

'I've burnt it.'

'Burnt it? When? I've always thought blackmailers never
destroy papers.'

'I burnt it a few hours ago. It made interesting reading.
Do you know what?'

'What?'

'You're going to sign my statement.' He opened a drawer
of the desk and taking out a fair-sized revolver placed it
before him.

I said, 'You won't get away with two murders.'

He said, 'There's ways of going about a job like that, and
there's ways of putting the remains out of sight.'

'A gun makes a lot of noise on this island,' I said. 'It
echoes all over the place.'

'O.K., it makes a lot of noise. Who's going to hear it?'

'Jimmie is not deaf.'

'No, but he's dumb. I'll see to it that he's dumb for
the rest of his life. No one squeals once Tom Wells says
they're dumb. And as for the boy – well, I'll settle with

anyone that tries to make evidence of what that half-wit says.'

I started to retreat. He stood up. 'Listen, honey. I don't want to do you any harm. There's no need to get alarmed. You'll sign my statement, it's for your own good. And I just want to warn you, if there's any retraction when you get home, I've got my boys in London. They can pay you a visit. I just want you to know, honey, that you'd better see my way of things.'

'I must find Jimmie,' I said, backing slowly out of the door.

'Naturally,' he said, 'of course. By all means talk it over with the boy-friend. He's got the right slant, he'll tell you the same as I've done.'

I was half-way out of the doorway when he said, 'You'll find him in the cellar. I've put him to crating the wines and liquor ready to take away. No use leaving that good stuff on the island.'

'Then I'll need the torch,' I said.

'That's right,' he said. He lifted the flashlamp off the window ledge and handed it to me. 'Don't break your neck down the steps, we don't want two corpses. Go and talk to Jimmie, dear.'

I slipped out by way of the storehouse, and made my way through the film of blue rising vapour down the mountain path again and, retrieving my parcel, continued my way along the beach to the aperture in the cliff which concealed the mouth of the tunnel.

I coughed my way through the sulphurous dust, my cough echoing on the walls of the cave, as if there were three or four people ahead of me, three or four behind. Twice I slipped on the slimy weeds, once scraping my elbow badly, but hardly noticing it in my efforts to make progress. My flashlamp cast a red glare in the volcanic dust. I came to that part of the tunnel where it dwindled to a hole, and I was obliged to crawl along the muddy floor with the parcel between my teeth. At last the cave widened, but it was low; I was forced to stoop and clutch the jutting shelves to assist my advance. It was here I looked for a suitable hiding-place for the journal, feeling with my hand the top surfaces of the protruding shelves, hoping to come across a flat rest. None of them had sufficient surface to retain my flat parcel, but running my hand over the upper face of a ledge I found that it fell back into a hole in the rock. I had to bend the parcel to squeeze it in.

My next plan was to return to the house, avoiding Wells if possible, and find Jimmie. If this could be done before Wells discovered the disappearance of the journal it might be possible for us, supported by the Browning, to take Wells by surprise and place him under arrest.

It seemed the wisest course to turn and retrace my journey through the tunnel to the beach, since by this route there would be less chance of my being overcome by the mist than if I emerged higher up on the South Arm. I still hesitated to return through the tunnel, for I was quite near to the South Arm door and I felt a suffocating desire for open air. However, I crouched under the shelf where my journal lay concealed, and gathered up my strength for the return journey through the caves. What I hated most in anticipation was the few yards of crawling. After a few minutes I set off, stooping and clutching at the rocky protuberances; and when the tunnel closed in to the dimensions of a tube, I crawled through as quickly as possible. The moment I emerged into the wider walls I had a fit of coughing. My cough echoed around me and, as it seemed, a short distance ahead. My cough subsided a little but the echoes from the interior seemed stronger and more frequent than my cough itself. I held my breath for a few seconds; and hearing a choking cough approach me, I knew it was not an echo.

At that moment I saw the light of a flashlamp casting a weak pink glow. I flashed my stronger torch in that direction, and saw Tom Wells stumbling and slithering towards me. I turned to make my escape the way I had come. His voice, spluttered with coughs, followed me: 'Don't move or I'll shoot. Don't move there.' The cave coughed and echoed his words: 'Don't move there. There, there, there.' I put out my torch and, crouching low, I pressed sideways against the wall. His flashlamp found me as he approached. He held it in his left hand, while his right hand was poised, as I thought, with the pistol.

'Where's that book?'

'What book?'

'Your diary.'

'You burnt it. You told me so.'

My eye was on his right hand. By the dim light of his weak torch I saw that he was holding a knife, not a revolver.

'I took your tip,' he said. 'Guns make too much noise.'

I flashed on my light. He blinked, and while he did so I bashed the flashlamp hard into the pit of his stomach. He cried, slipped and fell backwards.

I crawled back through the terrible hole, emerging to stumble along towards the air, clutching carelessly at rock ledges, so that my hands and arms were torn. When at last I came out of the cave the mist had fallen. I took refuge in a shallow crater, and lay there for about twenty minutes, not caring that the mist was pouring over me. Presently I pulled myself stiffly out of the crater and made my way to the deserted mill. There I spent the night, for the fog was too thick to permit my finding my way to the house. I spent most of the night listening fitfully for a sound and watching the dense air fearfully from the broken windows. Eventually I fell asleep on the soaking floor.

It must have been about six in the morning when I heard a sound. The mist was unfurling and the sun had risen. Light footsteps came round from the back of the house. I was getting ready to run for it when Miguel appeared.

He said, 'Mr Tom has got a bad cold. He got lost in the mist. He fell and hurt his head.'

'Is he in the house?'

'Yes. He came home this morning early. He fell and hurt himself.'

'What are you doing here?'

'I came to look for you. Jimmie has been to the Furnace to look for you.'

'Is Jimmie at home now?'

'Yes. He's looking after Mr Tom. Mr Tom is sitting out in the sun with his feet up.'

'You are sure Jimmie is in the house?'

'Naturally,' said Miguel in the accents of his idol.

'All right, I'll come with you.'

He made to set off in the direction of the tunnel.

'No,' I said, 'I'd rather not go home that way.'

'It's quicker,' said Miguel.

'This way's nice,' I said.

'I like that way,' said Miguel.

'You go that way,' I said, 'and I'll go this.'

But he decided to accompany me, and on the way he chatted about how Mr Tom's ribs were better, because last night he had taken a walk. 'And I showed him,' said Miguel, 'the secret tunnel at the beach, and he went in all by himself. But afterwards he got lost in the mist.'

Jimmie was in the kitchen, mixing rum with hot water and sugar.

'Ah,' said Jimmie, 'I lose my nerves that you have been lost. Where have you lodged?'

I said, 'At the mill.'

'You lose your way?' said Jimmie. 'We are in great

desolation that you are endangered last night from the mist.'

'Wells came after me with a knife,' I said.

'Is not so!' said Jimmie.

'It's true,' I said. 'I believe he would have killed me if I hadn't pushed him over and got away.'

I sat down and started to cry.

Jimmie said, 'Is to go too far. I am a man of patience but is to go too far. I attend to this Wells for you.'

He tasted the rum posset and seemed to approve of it. Then he carried it out to the patio where Tom Wells was sitting in the sun, nursing himself among a lot of garments. I stood by the door and watched him take the drinks over to Wells. He threw the drink in Wells's face. Then he took from his pocket the baby Browning and pointed it at Wells's head.

'Jimmie!' I shouted. 'Don't shoot at his head!'

He pressed the trigger. Nothing happened, not even a click. He pressed the trigger again and again, looking angrily at the gun, giving no attention to its aim.

Wells so far overcame his surprise as to throw off the coats in which he was swaddled. The rum was still running down his face when he saw that Jimmie's pistol was not working. He swiped at Jimmie and got him above the eye. Jimmie threw down the pistol and hit him back; it was a dreadful thud on the mouth, and blood began to run down Wells's shirt. I wish I knew the technical terms for fights; for, thinking it over afterwards, this between Wells and Jimmie seemed to me rather professional. Jimmie hit fast, one hand after the other. Wells was slow, but more powerful. I retrieved the automatic from the ground. I think I had the feeling that the violence might set it off. I glanced at it, and saw that the safety-catch was still on.

Wells had been knocked over. He rose, shook his head violently, and faced Jimmie again, in readiness. Jimmie was beginning to look glaze-eyed and exhausted when Miguel came running on to the patio with a very strange look. He seemed not to notice the fight, and ran up to the two breath-less heaving men.

'Out of the way, boy,' said Wells.

But Miguel was already tugging his arm, and Wells seemed glad of the pause.

'What's the matter, child?' he said.

Miguel's eyes were round and startled.

'Robinson is looking at the memorial,' he said.

'What's that you say?' said Wells.

'What is?' said Jimmie.

Miguel pointed towards the mustard field. Even from my place by the door I could see a man's figure stooping, with his hands on his knees, to read the words on Robinson's memorial. He straightened up and started walking slowly up to the house. Thinner and more weary than before, he was none the less unmistakably Robinson.

Chapter 11

JIMMIE had to take the bottles out of the crates where they were stacked in the storehouse for shipment. All the bottles went back into the cellar. Slowly, and by request, Tom Wells rendered up the key of the armoury, three boxes of cigars, two shirts, a camera, the *Shorter Oxford English Dictionary*, a pair of ormulu vases, a Bible, and other surprising objects which lay in the packing case he had prepared to take away with him. All that week Robinson went about inquiring after his goods: where was this and that? And he sat in his study like a potentate receiving tribute as his possessions came flowing back to him. Jimmie gave back the will. I had Robinson's fat fountain-pen. He asked for that, of course.

He did not appear at all to see why he should explain his disappearance. As soon as I realized that he had gone by his own choice, my fury rose.

'You might have thought of Miguel. It was a mean trick to play on Miguel. It made him ill,' I said, three or perhaps four times during our last week on the island.

Robinson would sigh, 'One can only act according to one's capacity,' or 'Miguel is to go to school in any case. He has to leave me. It will be less difficult now.'

Once he said, 'Yours is, of course, the obvious view. Well, my actions are beyond the obvious range. It surely needs only that you should realize this, not that you should understand my actions.'

I replied, 'I chucked the antinomian pose when I was twenty. There's no such thing as a private morality.'

'Not for you. But for me, living on an island – I have a system.'

161

On another occasion he said, 'Normally, my life is regulated, it is a system. It was disrupted by your arrival.'

'Any system,' I said, 'which doesn't allow for the unexpected and the unwelcome is a rotten one.'

At last he said, 'Things mount up inside one, and then one has to perpetrate an outrage.'

Owing to the strangeness of our predicament, the touchiness of our minds, the qualities of the island, and perhaps the shock of our plane accident, we did not for a moment suspect what had really happened. The blood was lying about everywhere. Our minds were on the blood.

When I think of Robinson now, I think of him as a selfish but well-meaning eccentric, but during our last week on the island I felt violently against him: one, because he went about with a lofty air; two, as a reaction against my romantic conception of him when I had thought him dead; and, three, because I had caught a heavy cold on the night I had spent in the old mill. I thought, noble heretic indeed. But really, after all, it was his island, and he probably, at the start, had saved our lives.

Tom Wells, with his face and eyes bruised from the fight, took to bed the day Robinson returned, and stayed there all week. Robinson attempted to commission me to look after him. I refused. 'He might catch my cold.'

'Is humorous,' Jimmie pointed out.

Robinson showed little interest when Jimmie and I gave him a graphic account of our ordeals. Our story was illustrated by Jimmie's black eye and my hands which had been cut and scratched in the tunnel.

Robinson said, 'It was only to be expected.'

Once he said to me, 'Wells is complaining of stomach trouble through living on tinned food. That's your fault for depriving him of wildfowl and rabbit. You ought not to have locked up the guns.'

I said, 'We caught some fish.'

He said, 'That's insufficient diet for a man like Wells.'

'He would never have stirred himself to go shooting game.'

'Jimmie might have done so.'

'Jimmie knows nothing about guns.'

Then I noticed that Robinson was laughing silently to himself.

'Tom Wells nearly killed me,' I said.

'That would not have been serious for you,' he said. 'You've got to die some time.'

I felt there was a flaw in this argument, but because of my cold in the head I simply could not think how to refute it with dignity on the spot. Instead, I took another line: 'It would have been serious for Wells.'

'Yes, it would have been serious for Wells,' he said.

'And for me too,' I said then, 'for I'm not ready to die yet.'

Robinson would not be drawn into telling where he had concealed himself. When Jimmie told him of our long search he assumed the air of a triumphant schoolmistress.

Bit by bit we got the story out of Miguel, whose manner with Robinson was now rather restrained, and to whom Robinson, in the hope of regaining his confidence, had given an account of his late whereabouts.

A few weeks before his disappearance he had planned to leave us; he began to lay up stores for himself in the old smugglers' storehouse, of which he had told us, the cave called The Market. The last of these stores were conveyed from the house at the time when, some of our food having gone bad, he and Jimmie had made up packages for the Furnace. He managed to bamboozle Jimmie, which did not surprise me, and got some good stores away without suspicion.

The Market, lying among the sheer cliffs on the west coast of the South Arm, was quite inaccessible from the island.

'Have you ever seen The Market?' I asked Miguel.

'No, naturally.'

'How did Robinson get there with all his stores?'

'He took the little boat.'

A few days before Robinson's disappearance, he had been mending this boat with the aid of Jimmie.

'Did Robinson often go to The Market in the boat?'

'No, naturally. It's dangerous among the rocks, with a little boat.'

'I think I want my head examined,' Jimmie said, 'as I have assisted Robinson to mend this boat.'

'Yes,' I said, 'why didn't we think of the boat?'

'We were taking thought for the blood,' Jimmie said.

It was the blood which gave me to think of the well of darkness in Robinson's character. Of course, it was amusing in a sense, his having led the goat to the mountain, fired the shot for all to hear, without shooting the goat. He cut its throat a few days later in the mustard field, during the night of the second of July, had soaked in its blood everything he could lay hands on, and, dragging the carcass to the Furnace, had scattered the bloody evidence all along the path. I pictured how he had plastered goat's blood over our clothes, carefully omitting those of Tom Wells and Miguel. I could not deny the comic element, at the same time as I could not help thinking, there is something vicious in him. What urged him to make such a display of blood? Why? What bloody delight was satisfied?

Once, in my presence, Ian Brodie telephoned to Curly Lonsdale to tell him, confidentially, that Julia had cancer of the womb. I knew that Julia had been rather unwell, but this was the first I had heard of cancer. I gasped, and looked at Agnes. She was sitting fatly in the chair, giggling quietly to herself. Agnes always abetted her husband in his practical jokes, as unconscious of her motives in this as she was in her habit of giving Ian for birthdays and Christmas photographic books of 'art studies' – that is, representations of nude girls, and making no secret of it, for wasn't it art?

'Nothing much,' Ian Brodie said into the telephone, 'to worry about, only cancer of the womb.' I thought, 'What's Julia to him? What cancer of the soul is venting itself?'

All through that week Jimmie continued to press garrulously upon Robinson the details of what had occurred during his absence. Robinson would usually reply, 'It was only to be expected.' I found this phrase unendurable with its implication that he had foreseen all the consequences of his action to the last detail, and that he more or less held the wires that made us move.

Towards the end of the week I said to Robinson, 'I believe Tom Wells is a professional blackmailer.'

'You are full of suspicions,' he said.

'What about his trying to blackmail Jimmie and me?' I said.

'That does not prove him a professional.'

'I think those documents he missed from his bag were to do with blackmail.'

'In fact,' said Robinson, 'they were obscene photographs. I burnt them.'

'He's a criminal type,' I said.

'You are full of suspicions. You thought he had murdered me, and you were wrong.'

'Not far wrong. He tried to kill me.'

'It was only to be expected.'

I turned on him. I said, 'What do you mean, it was only to be expected.'

He sighed, and I could have thrown something at him for it.

'Generally,' he said, 'people act in this way. Human nature does not vary much. It was to be expected that a

165

man like Wells would turn a situation to his own interests. It was to be expected that a woman like you would, in the circumstances, withdraw very rapidly from a man like Jimmie.'

'That was the reason!' I said.

He looked troubled. 'What reason for what?'

'Your reason for arranging this farce – it was to separate Jimmie and me. You need not have bothered, I'm quite capable of judging for myself –'

'I don't want you to think – I mean, you never know where these things may lead.'

'It would never do,' I said, 'to keep a disorderly island.'

He said, 'I don't want you to think that I had nothing else in mind but your relationship with Jimmie when I decided to leave. Motives are seldom simple. I find no call upon me to go into my motives. Of course, you are annoyed. It is only to be expected.'

I said, 'I have taught the child the rosary.'

He said, 'I didn't think you would do that.'

I said, 'It was only to be expected. I made a very nice rosary for him from the amber beads among the salvage.'

'The salvage is not your property,' he said helplessly.

'There was no one to guard the salvage and so I helped myself. It was only to be –'

'Miguel's religion was not your business,' he said.

'True,' I said, 'it was yours. But I charge no fee.'

'Did you do this to revenge yourself in some way? What exactly was your reason? That you wanted to gain influence over the boy? Was it to feed your possessive instincts? Some unconscious urge? Was it –'

'I see no call to tear myself to bits over motives,' I said. 'They are never simple. I am happy to say I have taught the child the rosary.'

'What else have you taught him? Have you put something

166

against me into his mind? He has been strange with me since my return.'

'You are full of suspicions,' I said.

'Miguel is not the same,' he said.

'If you choose to depart in a sudden shower of blood, leaving him with strangers, he will of course have reservations on your return. It is only to be expected.'

'He will forget the rosary,' said Robinson, 'in time.'

I said, 'He wants to go to a Catholic school.'

'You have been really hostile to my intentions,' Robinson said.

'In fact,' I said, 'it was Jimmie who put the idea into his head.' This was true. Often, in the course of entertaining Miguel with stories about his schooldays in a priory, Jimmie had advised, 'Is best to go to a Catholic school. Is more strict and terrible than any other, and in consequence is more delight and joy to infringe the rules.'

'I shall be glad,' said Robinson, 'to see the pomegranate boat.'

On the late afternoon of Sunday, the eighth of August, the pomegranate men spilt ashore. It was strange to see so many people, to hear so many voices, and all talking at once. They were highly intrigued and puzzled by the memorial, which Robinson had refused to let Jimmie dismantle.

I had vaguely imagined that the pomegranate boat would take us aboard and set off with us. Instead, they sent wireless messages, and early next morning three planes circled the island, dipped low and disappeared. Another plane arrived. Robinson sent up his kite from the flat pastureland of the West Leg, and there, as the plane made to land, Robinson drew it in again, like a fluttering red bird coming wearily to roost.

Robinson handed to Tom Wells a cardboard box which, it transpired, contained his lucky charms. 'Thanks a lot,' said Wells. He was grinning to right and left. He grimaced at me, 'I hope we're going to let bygones be bygones.' I stooped to stroke the cat.

My journal, which Miguel had retrieved from the tunnel and which was still wrapped in the piece of Robinson's waterproof, was my only luggage.

Before we left, Robinson asked me if I would like to take the cat home with me. I half thought this was an ironic question, since Bluebell now took hardly any notice of Robinson. But he went on to explain that he would be leaving the island for a few weeks with the pomegranate boat, in order to take Miguel to school. He could not leave the cat on the island, and the pomegranate boat was already equipped with a cat. He would be obliged if I would accept the gift of Bluebell if I didn't mind waiting for the period of quarantine.

He also gave me a print of the photograph of the stream gushing from the cactus, which he had taken on the mountain.

Chapter 12

I STARED at what Julia was carrying. She became aware of my attention; then, embarrassed by a sudden recollection, tucked it away under her arm. It was my real crocodile leather handbag, left to me by my grandmother.

'Of course, you understand, your house is up for sale,' said Agnes.

Curly's car splashed through the downpour, carrying us from the airport. 'Take it from me, she doesn't want to talk business now,' said Curly.

I sat between Brian and Julia at the back. Julia whispered, 'We would have had a lot of business trouble with your affairs. I've had a lot of trouble with Agnes. It was foolish of you to die intestate. You'd better make a will in case it happens again.'

Brian fairly rocked.

'What's the joke back there?' said Curly.

I said, 'Julia wants me to make a will.'

'So you should,' said Agnes.

'In the name of God,' said Curly, 'can't you talk about something more cheerful? This is an occasion, it's an occasion.'

Tom Wells gave the exclusive story to a Sunday paper the following week, whether in his own words or not makes little difference.

> What's it like to be an island castaway?
> To come face to face with the Alone? . . .
> To endure the agony of loneliness, know-
> ing that the folks at home have given up
> hope? . . .

A Family Man

Mind you, it was hard work to keep alive. *It was a constant contest with Nature and Death.* ... My one thought was for my wife. ... Jan was the only woman among us three men, and naturally there might have been some awkward situations. I'm a family man myself. But I saw to it from the start that *the strictest proprieties were observed.* Nights, it was oh so lonely ...

True Comradeship

Those three months were stark, grim, challenging, but I wouldn't have missed them for worlds. *I never knew what true comradeship was till I lived on that island.* Everyone pulled his or her weight. ...

That Lucky Charm. ...

I happened to have on me a lucky charm, just a tiny metal object of ancient Druid design. It's my firm conviction that *I owe it to that lucky charm.* ...

We never had a moment's disagreement. ...

Of course, it was a strain on Jan's nerves, but she was a brick. ...

Would that I were, I thought, and I would hurl myself at his fat head.

I was staying with Julia and Curly until my house should be put to rights again. I wondered however I could have thought of Tom Wells bearing any likeness to Curly. And the facial resemblance now seemed to me super-ficial – Curly had a way of opening out his face expectantly to the world, which might be difficult to live with all the time, but differed from Tom Wells's open-mouthed regard, so like that of a dew-lapped dog forever wanting a drink.

'I suppose you'll want to sleep late in the mornings?' Julia had inquired dolefully.

'Naturally, naturally,' said Curly. 'After what she's been through she's got to take it easy.'

And when he paddled upstairs with my breakfast tray every morning, and when I heard his voice at the street door discouraging the reporters with terse unprintable phrases, I thought him the kindest of all my relatives.

'Alas, is never that I have luck with the English ladies,' Jimmie had said while we waited for our separate planes in the hotel at Lisbon. 'In the time of the end of the hostilities I have fallen in love with an English lady who is driving the car of a colonel in France. This lady is of noble blood, and she has declared to me, "I am not yet old enough to marry without the permission of my pa, but I go on leave to my home and I tell of you to pa. Mayhaps he should desire to meet you, and lo! he shall permit the marriage." Now I say to this lady, "What is about the ma?" and she has replied, "Ma has married to another; is necessary only to fix pa." Alas, then this lady departs to England, and she is writing to me most woeful because the faulty old pa has the plan for his daughter to marry a great lord or mayhaps an American. Then lo! I have a visitor. Is the brother of my lady love, a captain of the English Army. He has declared to me, "Behold, is five hundred pounds, and you bloody well lay off the girl."'

Jimmie sat back in his chair and despondently sipped his brandy and soda. 'Is never any luck with English girls. Is my destiny,' he concluded.

'What happened about this girl? Did you see her again?'

'Never. From that day I cease to write letters to that lady.'

'Did you refuse the five hundred?'

'No, no; on the contrary, I settle for six hundred and fifty. This cash is necessary for my expenses along about that time.'

'Many a man,' I said admiringly, 'would have taken the money *and* the girl.'

'Is to go too far. I am a man of honour,' said Jimmie, 'wherefore is mayhaps the reason that I do not have luck with English ladies.'

'I should think,' said Ian Brodie, 'you were in your element with three men dancing round you, and no other woman around.'

'It was delightful,' I said.

'Nice chaps, were they?'

'Charming.'

'This Robinson seems a peculiar sort, living like that on an island. I don't like the sound of *him*.'

'He was delightful,' I said.

'Oh, was he?'

'Yes, charming.'

'There was a young boy. Supposed to be adopted.'

'Yes, charming.'

'It must have been awkward, all living together like that.'

'It was delightful,' I said, 'it was charming.'

'Well,' he said, 'it's rather embarrassing for me, you know, when people ask what happened.'

'Don't they read the papers?'

'There's always a lot more behind these things – people want to know what really happened.'

'Oh, it was really, tell them, all delightful and charming.'

'What I can't understand is why Brian preferred to stay with the Lonsdales. . . .'

Gradually most of my possessions were returned to me.

Sometimes I wondered what happened to my six pairs of nylons. Agnes returned two pairs of gloves. Ian Brodie had already sold some of my books.

Green-eyes Bluebell came out of quarantine within six months. After the first two lessons her memory of ping-pong returned. By this time I was once more settled in Chelsea.

One day, when Brian was telling me how news of the plane crash had arrived, and how, after a week, we were despaired of, he remarked, with his slightly alarming sophistication, 'It's difficult for the young, those without experience of life, to realize death.'

In the autumn of 1955 I read, under the title 'Island Man in Dock,' the case of Tom Wells which was heard at the Old Bailey. He was described as the director of Luck Unlimited Ltd, a firm of wholesalers dealing in lucky charms and medals, and as proprietor of the monthly magazine *Your Future*. Charged with uttering letters of blackmail against an unnamed couple, he pleaded guilty, and asked for twenty-three other charges to be taken into consideration. Plus two more, I thought.

The defending counsel recalled that Mr Wells had undergone a severe nervous strain after a plane crash in which he had sustained serious injuries, and was subsequently exiled on a desert island, where, for three months, he endured pain, hunger and thirst. Mr Wells's business affairs had suffered a severe set-back during his absence and since his return he had also had domestic troubles. Throughout the past twenty years, and in the course of his editorship of *Your Future*, involving a large correspondence of an intimate nature, Mr Wells had given valuable advice and brought comfort to many thousands. Bearing these factors in mind, it was hoped that a lenient view would be taken of Mr Wells's having yielded to the more than usual temptations with which his work presented him.

The prosecution said it was one of the nastiest cases ever to come before those courts. 'In any sense – *nasty*.' Over a period of ten years – stretching back, that was, to a period long preceding his escape from the plane disaster – the accused had been extorting money from men and women who had, in their innocence, confided their most cherished secrets, the deepest anguish of their souls, to Wells. Operating under the name of Dr Benignus, Wells had solicited such confidences through the columns of his paper. The court would agree that *benign* was the very last word one could apply . . . .

He got seven years. Two of his associates, a woman secretary charged with aiding and abetting, and a man, said to be in the pay of Wells, charged with trespassing with intent to intimidate, got three and five years respectively.

I supposed that only Miguel would be sorry.

Next spring I learned from a news paragraph in an evening paper that the island was sinking.

'Robinson', the tiny man-shaped Atlantic island owned by the recluse Mr M. M. Robinson, is sinking, say experts.

Within three years, it is estimated, the topmost point of the 3,000-ft. mountain will disappear under the sea. Already the sea level has risen over twenty feet, and a strip of white beach on the south coast, which was the pride of the island, is now under water. The event is explained by volcanic action.

Mr Robinson is already making plans for evacuation.

It will be recalled that a plane bound for the Azores crashed on 'Robinson' in May 1954, the survivors of which . . .

In a sense I had already come to think of the island as a place of the mind. I opened up once more the blue exercise book wrapped in the square from Robinson's waterproof, still smelling so of sulphur that for a moment I was crawling again in the cave with the parcel between my teeth.

It is now, indeed, an apocryphal island. It may be a trick

of the mind to sink one's past fear and exasperation in the waters of memory; it may be a truth of the mind.

From time to time since I read this news I have pictured Robinson wearily moving his possessions on to some boat bound for some other isolation. I have thought greedily of the books. And of Miguel, wondering if they think him backward at his school in Lisbon.

And now, perhaps it is because the island is passing out of sight that it rises so high in my thoughts. Even while the journal brings before me the events of which I have written, they are transformed, there is undoubtedly a sea-change, so that the island resembles a locality of childhood, both dangerous and lyrical. I have impressions of the island of which I have not told you, and could not entirely if I had a hundred tongues – the mustard field staring at me with its yellow eye, the blue and green lake seeing in me a hard turquoise stone, the goat's blood observing me red, guilty, all red. And sometimes when I am walking down the King's Road or sipping my espresso in the morning – feeling, not old exactly, but fussy and adult – and chance to remember the island, immediately all things are possible.

Muriel Spark

'Far and away our best woman novelist' – Penelope Mortimer

THE BALLAD OF PECKHAM RYE

An entertaining tale of satanism in South London.

THE PRIME OF MISS JEAN BRODIE

When an unbridled schoolmistress with advanced ideas is in her prime no one (except Muriel Spark) can predict what will happen.

MEMENTO MORI

Evelyn Waugh has called this account of the duplicities and self-deceptions in the past and present lives of a group of elderly people 'a brilliant and singularly gruesome achievement'.

THE MANDELBAUM GATE

A girl's pilgrimage to Jordan becomes a flight . . . a desperate adventure of abduction and espionage ... . a love story sacred and profane . . .

THE COMFORTERS

A riotous cast of Catholics and neurotics makes her first novel 'brilliantly original and fascinating' – Evelyn Waugh

and

THE BACHELORS

THE DRIVER'S SEAT

THE GIRLS OF SLENDER MEANS

THE GO-AWAY BIRD AND OTHER STORIES

THE PUBLIC IMAGE